TALES THE COUNTESS TOLD

A play for the stage
about the life and fairy tales
of the Countess d'Aulnoy

By
STEPHEN WYATT

MARIE-CATHERINE LE JUMEL DE BARNEVILLE,
COMTESSE D'AULNOY
(1650 – 1705)
"The most famous French writer of fairy stories after Perrault"
(The Oxford Companion to Fairy Tales)

Copyright Stephen Wyatt

All the rights are reserved.

Any enquiries regarding performance or reproduction
should be addressed to the author's agents:
Valerie Hoskins Associates,
20, Charlotte Street,
London W1P 1HJ
Telephone (020) 76374490

ISBN 978-0-9556868-7-0

Characters

THE COUNTESS
LOUISE
THE STEWARD
PHILIPPE

THE CREATURES OF THE COUNTESS'S IMAGINATION

SETTING: THE COUNTESS'S GARDEN

NOTE ON THE STAGING

The suggestions for staging are only suggestions.
The whole piece is intended as an invitation to the theatrical imagination.

PART ONE

(DARKNESS. A CLAP OF THUNDER.)
(THE EARTHQUAKE MUSIC FROM RAMEAU'S *LES INDES GALANTES*.)
(A LIGHTNING FLASH SHOWS THE SILHOUETTE OF AN IMPERIOUS BEWIGGED FIGURE MAKING A GESTURE OF BANISHMENT.)
(THE COUNTESS'S VOICE IS HEARD IN THE BLACKNESS:)

COUNTESS: Now the King was very angry and he looked everywhere for someone to blame. And, of course, he thought of the Countess. But the Countess had become older and wiser. Instead of waiting for a summons to the presence of the angry King, she decided to pack her bags and seek solace in the sleepy realms of Arcadia.

(THE EARTHQUAKE MUSIC STARTS TO SUBSIDE. THE ROYAL FIGURE STARTS TO FADE BACK INTO THE DARK. GRADUALLY PASTORAL MUSIC – RAMEAU AGAIN – STARTS TO SEEP IN)

(THE LIGHTS COME UP SLOWLY ON A STRANGE MAGICAL GARDEN, PART SEVENTEENTH FORMAL WITH CLASSICAL STATUARY, PART A WILDERNESS OF BRIGHT, EXOTIC VEGETATION, MADE UP OF A DISCONCERTING MIX OF FOLIAGE AND HALF HIDDEN HUMAN BEINGS. THE MUSIC FADES.)

(THE COUNTESS SITS IN THE GARDEN, A HALF WRITTEN LETTER IN HER HAND, LOST IN THOUGHT.)
(A SHEEP BLEATS)
(SHE TURNS ON IT IN FURY.)

COUNTESS: Baa! Baaaa! Baaaaa! Baaaaaa!!!

(THE SHEEP IS SILENCED. THE COUNTESS RETURNS TO HER LETTER, RE-READING WHAT SHE'S WRITTEN.)

COUNTESS: My dear Eloise, do you remember that time in our salon when we all discussed the merits of country life – its tranquillity, its honesty, its closeness to nature? I seem to remember I waxed eloquent on the subject of my own dear Barneville where I was born and brought up. But now I know the truth. A few days here in Barneville is a delight, an idyll. A few months in Barneville is a form of torture.

(A PAUSE. THEN SHE STARTS TO WRITE.)

COUNTESS: Many thanks for your news from Paris. I know you can tell me nothing of the matter which most concerns me – but I fear I have become like a starving dog skulking under the table – I am ravenous for even the merest scrap of gossip.

(THE SHEEP BLEATS. SHE GIVES IT A FILTHY LOOK.)

COUNTESS: For all I know the sheep here cherish any number of dark guilty secrets inside their woolly heads. But not being a sheep myself, I have no access to all the ovine gossip.

(THE COUNTESS'S STEWARD ENTERS.)

STEWARD: (HESITANTLY) My lady –
COUNTESS: (LOOKING UP) No, don't tell me –
STEWARD: The carriage you ordered for this afternoon –
COUNTESS: Is still broken down. The blacksmith has not yet mended the axle.
STEWARD: The axle is there, my lady, and fitted.
COUNTESS: You don't mean that it is going to be possible finally for me to take a drive in the country?
STEWARD: No, my lady. The black horse –
COUNTESS: Has lost a shoe?
STEWARD: Has sprained its fetlock.
COUNTESS: Which means - ?
STEWARD: The black horse will not be fit to pull your carriage for another couple of weeks.
COUNTESS: And there is no other suitable horse?
STEWARD: No, my lady.
COUNTESS: Why did I know that?
STEWARD: I'm very sorry, my lady.
COUNTESS: I'm sure the two weeks will pass by in the blinking of an eye. You may go.
STEWARD: Thank you, my lady.

(THE STEWARD BOWS AND LEAVES. THE COUNTESS GIVES A SIGH OF SUPPRESSED EXASPERATION. THEN RETURNS TO HER LETTER)

COUNTESS: (WRITING) It is not possible to convey the snail like pace of life here. Taking my carriage out requires complex negotiation and if I rage, things go more slowly still. A day is an age – the cows moo, the sheep bleat, the horses whinny, my steward makes excuses for doing nothing. Of course, I try to write. But somehow Barneville reduces the fount of inspiration to a feeble muddy trickle.

(PAUSE)

What I lack more than anything is an audience. If only you were here – or I was back in Paris reading aloud to my friends in the salon. Exile was the safe option. But I'm not sure now whether it isn't a greater punishment than anything his majesty could think of.

(ALMOST IMPERCEPTIBLY THE GARDEN STARTS TO MOVE.)

COUNTESS: If I could have a wish, this is what it would be. I want someone to talk to, a companion, a kindred spirit. I have as much chance of finding such a person here as of encountering a beached whale. But then – I remember you telling me that I was a witch. If I set my mind to wishing for something I was always sure to get it in the end. And I reminded you that I write fairy stories. And in fairy stories having a wish granted is not usually an unmixed blessing. But still – what do I have to lose?

(SHE CLOSES HER EYES.)

COUNTESS: I wish… I wish…

(THE GARDEN BECOMES MORE AGITATED. MUSIC CREEPS SOFTLY IN – THE ENTRY OF POLYMNIE FROM RAMEAU'S *LES BOREADES*.)
(THE STEWARD RE-ENTERS.)
(HE GIVES A DISCREET COUGH. THE COUNTESS OPENS HER EYES. THE MUSIC SLOWLY FADES. THE GARDEN CEASES ITS MOTION.)

STEWARD: Excuse me, my lady -
COUNTESS: Yes?
STEWARD: There's a young gentlewoman asking to see you.
COUNTESS: (SLOWLY) A young gentlewoman?
STEWARD: Yes, she says she is your neighbour.
COUNTESS: Her name?
STEWARD: Madame de Ventadour.
COUNTESS: And she really arrived just now – unannounced.
STEWARD: She was most apologetic. She said that she hoped she might be forgiven for the unexpected intrusion.
COUNTESS: Forgiven? Thanked more like.
STEWARD: Shall I admit here?
COUNTESS: Of course.

(THE STEWARD LEAVES. THE COUNTESS TAKES UP HER PEN.)

COUNTESS: My dear Eloise, the most extraordinary thing. I – (PUTTING DOWN HER PEN) No, no, don't break the spell.

(THE STEWARD USHERS IN LOUISE DE VENTADOUR THEN LEAVES. THE COUNTESS RISES TO GREET HER. LOUISE IS YOUNG AND NERVOUS.)

COUNTESS: My dear Madame de Ventadour, welcome.

(SHE GESTURES FOR LOUISE TO SIT. LOUISE STILL TONGUE-TIED SITS BY HER SIDE.)

LOUISE: I feel quite embarrassed at my boldness in intruding in this way. I have seen your house in the distance on a number of occasions when I have been out in my carriage and I have to confess since we are neighbours I have often wanted to make your acquaintance.
COUNTESS: You are lonely.
LOUISE: (THROWN BY THE BLUNTNESS) Yes, I suppose I am.
COUNTESS: And your husband?
LOUISE: He is often away. He likes to hunt.
COUNTESS: Deer? Boar? Other women?
LOUISE: I – I would not think ill of my husband.
COUNTESS: No, of course not. Forgive me. I have become a very inquisitive old woman.
LOUISE: Hardly old, madame.
COUNTESS: Old enough to be your mother.
LOUISE: My mother is not old, Madame.
COUNTESS: A good answer. Well done!

(PAUSE.)

COUNTESS: What is your name, child?
LOUISE: Louise, Madame.
COUNTESS: My dear Louise, delightful though your visit is to me, I have to ask you – do you know who I am?
LOUISE: You are my neighbour, Madame – and a lady of quality I feel confident I am privileged to visit.
COUNTESS: So your husband has said nothing?
LOUISE: Forgive me, I don't understand.
COUNTESS: I am Marie-Catherine Le Jumel de Barneville, Countess d'Aulnoy.

(AN IMPRESSIVE PAUSE.)

COUNTESS: The name means nothing to you?
LOUISE: (APOLOGETICALLY) No, madame.

COUNTESS:	Well, thank heaven for that. (PAUSE) How old are you, my dear?
LOUISE:	Eighteen.
COUNTESS:	And your husband?
LOUISE:	He is forty-five, Madame.
COUNTESS:	A father figure?
LOUISE:	He is my husband.
COUNTESS:	Just so. And you were married…?
LOUISE:	When I was seventeen.
COUNTESS:	Ah - I was married at sixteen.
LOUISE:	But, Madame, seventeen is only-
COUNTESS:	I know, I know. But by your age I was in the Bastille on trial for conspiracy to murder my husband.
LOUISE:	(SHOCKED) Madame, I-
COUNTESS:	What?
LOUISE:	I - I'm sure you were wrongfully accused.
COUNTESS:	Alas, no. I did everything I could to see him dead. Unfortunately, I failed.
LOUISE:	(STARTING TO RISE) Madame, I-
COUNTESS:	You ought to go? Is that what you mean?
LOUISE:	I don't wish to appear impolite but-
COUNTESS:	You see why I asked about your husband. He is of an age to remember the Countess d'Aulnoy - and thoroughly disapprove.

(A PAUSE. THEN LOUISE SITS DOWN AGAIN)

LOUISE:	(FIRMLY) Madame, I am a guest in your house and I am sure that whatever happened, you had good reasons for what you did.
COUNTESS:	(GENUINELY IMPRESSED) My dear, I think I shall like you after all. But I don't want you to fall out with your husband on my account.
LOUISE:	My husband is a man of great soul.
COUNTESS:	(DRYLY) Then you are a remarkably fortunate young bride.
LOUISE:	(HOTLY) Yes, I think I am.
COUNTESS:	But there is something else I should warn you about.
LOUISE:	Surely not, Madame.
COUNTESS:	I am beyond the pale in another way. I write fairy stories
LOUISE:	I don't understand.
COUNTESS:	I am one of those dangerous women who hold salons in Paris and read the stories they have written out loud.
LOUISE:	(THOUGHTFULLY) You write stories.
COUNTESS:	My dear, I do not understand your emphasis.
LOUISE:	I'm sorry - but you said stories –
COUNTESS:	Yes, fairy stories.
LOUISE:	Well, of course, my nurse used to tell me fairy stories when I was young-
COUNTESS:	Your nurse told you country tales. Without shape, without artistry. Mine are very different.
LOUISE:	I used to love listening to her.

COUNTESS:	I am not condemning you, my dear. Or your nurse. I do not wish to boast but the tales I tell are read out in the most fashionable salons in the whole of Paris. They are not nursery tales.
LOUISE:	I am being stupid.
COUNTESS:	Louise, you are far from stupid. But I am describing something you have not encountered.
LOUISE:	Would you tell me one of your stories?
COUNTESS:	Of course – with the greatest of pleasure. If you're sure you want to listen.
LOUISE:	I'd like to listen – very much. I am not expected home for some hours. And if I hear your tale, I will perhaps learn more about you.
COUNTESS:	Perhaps.
LOUISE:	Did you really plot to murder your husband?
COUNTESS:	Oh yes. (PAUSE) Is that what you want me to tell you about?
LOUISE:	Not at all. I'd much prefer the fairy story but-
COUNTESS:	My dear, relax – just listen and be patient. As you said yourself, you may learn something.
LOUISE:	Does your story have a moral then?
COUNTESS:	Nothing as straightforward as that. But instructive nevertheless. (PAUSE) Well, are you ready?
LOUISE:	Of course.

(SUDDENLY THE GARDEN IS IN A STATE OF VIOLENT AGITATION. FIGURES MOVE, FOLIAGE SHAKES. TRUMPETS RING OUT – THE OPENING FANFARE FROM OVERTURE TO RAMEAU'S *LES PALADINS*. THE LIGHTS FADE DOWN ON THE GARDEN ISOLATING THE COUNTESS AND LOUISE.)

COUNTESS: I call this - the story of Princess Laidronette and the Green Serpent. Once upon a time there was a great queen who gave birth to twins – both daughters, both beautiful. So she invited twelve fairies who lived nearby to the christening to bestow gifts upon them, as was the custom in those days.

(FROM THE DARKNESS OF THE GARDEN A CRADLE AND A LINE OF SMALL FAIRIES APPEAR FLUTTERING ABOVE IT.)

COUNTESS: Unfortunately, the queen made a fatal miscalculation – as fairy tale rulers are inclined to do, unlike, of course, their real life equivalents. She forgot to invite the fairy Magotine.

(A CLAP OF THUNDER. A MAD CACKLE. THE QUEEN CONFRONTS THE EVIL FAIRY MAGOTINE.)

QUEEN:	(TAKING A DEEP BREATH) Fairy Magotine, delighted that you can make it. Please be good enough to take your seat at the table.
MAGOTINE:	(OMINOUSLY SOFT) Your majesty, if you had really wanted me to take a seat at your table, you would have sent me an invitation. But you only want fairies who are young and pretty. You didn't want Magotine because she is ugly and old. Now where are those two precious little darlings?

(SHE HURRIES OVER TO THE CRADLE AND PICKS UP ONE OF THE BABIES WITHIN. THE BABY CRIES)

MAGOTINE:	Well, little girl, I'll make sure you never forget the Fairy Magotine. (CACKLING) I endow you with – perfect ugliness!
QUEEN:	No! No!
MAGOTINE:	Oh yes, you will be ugly – for ever! And as for her little sister –
QUEEN:	Stop – stop – assist me, fairies!

(AS MAGOTINE REACHES FOR THE SECOND BABY, THE QUEEN WRENCHES THE FIRST CHILD FROM HER HANDS.)

MAGOTINE:	Oh very well, if my fairy sisterhood insists. To curse one child is sufficient. To curse two, simply greedy.

(SHE GIVES HER WICKED CACKLE AND DISAPPEARS FROM SIGHT, LEAVING THE QUEEN CLASPING HER BABY. IT STARTS TO CRY AGAIN)

QUEEN:	There, there, my darling –
COUNTESS:	But as the horrified Queen took the first infant in her arms, she watched her grow uglier and uglier by the minute…
QUEEN:	She – she is becoming hideous. I can hardly bear to look at her. (BECOMING INCREASINGLY HYSTERICAL) What is happening? My beautiful baby – she's hideous, she's hideous! Take her away! I can't bear the sight of her!

(SHE HOLDS UP THE BABY IN ANGUISH AS SHE DISAPPEARS INTO THE DARKNESS.)

COUNTESS:	Well, of course, the babies grew in time into young women. The queen called her elder daughter Laidronette and the younger Bellotte. These names suited them perfectly for Laidronette, despite her boundless intelligence, was as ugly as sin and getting uglier - while her sister's beauty increased daily.
LOUISE:	Madame –
COUNTESS:	(BREAKING OFF) What is it, my dear?
LOUISE:	Why was the Princess cursed with ugliness?
COUNTESS:	It was her fate.
LOUISE:	So she wasn't being punished?

COUNTESS:	Not for anything she'd done, no.
LOUISE:	And her sister – she became more and more beautiful without having done anything to deserve it?
COUNTESS:	That was her fate.
LOUISE:	Isn't it all rather unfair?
COUNTESS:	Of course. But then – isn't life?
LOUISE:	And the Queen – was she married?
COUNTESS:	Oh yes, there was a King.
LOUISE:	Then I'm surprised you didn't mention him. Was he-
COUNTESS:	(GENTLY) My dear, if you keep on asking questions, I fear we'll never get to the end of the story.

(IN THE DIM LIGHT THE GARDEN IS AGAIN IN MOTION.)

COUNTESS: When the Princess Bellotte was fifteen, she was engaged to be married to the handsome son of a neighbouring King. The Princess Laidronette who had been living in self-imposed seclusion for the last few years turned up – to her mother's dismay.

(OUT OF THE DARKNESS, THE QUEEN EMERGES TO CONFRONT HER DAUGHTER, WHO CARRIES A MASK OF INFINITE UGLINESS OVER HER FACE.)

QUEEN:	(UNPLEASANTLY SURPRISED) Laidronette –
LAIDRONETTE:	Mother-
QUEEN:	We hadn't expected to see you. I'm afraid you've grown a great deal uglier since I last saw you.
LAIDRONETTE:	I did so want to see my sister's wedding.
QUEEN:	Well, of course, you can see it, dear.
LAIDRONETTE:	(JOYFULLY) Oh thank you, mother!
QUEEN:	I'm sure we can find some screen for you to stand behind with a hole for you to peep through.

(THE QUEEN LEAVES. LAIDRONETTE STANDS THERE STUNNED AND UNMOVING.)

COUNTESS: The Princess Laidronette watched the wedding from behind her screen and then left the palace. She knew in her heart of hearts that she was so hideous that even her own mother was relieved to see the back of her.

(THE PRINCESS STARTS TO MOVE.)

COUNTESS: She walked deep into the forest. Although she tried not to be bitter, she felt the heart inside her shrivelling like a leaf in autumn.

	(A DEEP DARK FOREST. FOREST WHISPERINGS. AS SHE WALKS THROUGH, LAIDRONETTE GIVES A HEART FELT SIGH. THEN A RUSTLING NOISE.
LAIDRONETTE:	Who's there?
	(FURTHER RUSTLING. THEN A SUDDEN HISS. LAIDRONETTE STOPS IN HORROR. A WRITHING GREEN SERPENT CONFRONTS HER.)
COUNTESS:	A long, long green serpent confronted her, its hideous length curled round the foot of a tree.
	(LAIDRONETTE STANDS MESMERISED.)
LAIDRONETTE:	Don't hurt me – please.
SERPENT:	Why should I hurt you?
LAIDRONETTE:	You're a serpent and-
SERPENT:	I'm horrible to look at?
LAIDRONETTE:	Yes, but-
SERPENT:	Laidronette, you're not the only unhappy creature. At birth I was even handsomer than you. Listen to me-
LAIDRONETTE:	(STARTING TO RUN) No! Leave me alone! No! No! No!
	(THE PRINCESS AND THE SERPENT DISAPPEAR INTO THE BLACKNESS.)
COUNTESS:	The Princess fled from the serpent's ugly green coils in terror.
LOUISE:	Excuse me, Madame-
COUNTESS:	Yes?
LOUISE:	How did it come about that the serpent could speak?
COUNTESS:	You mean you've never met a snake which could talk?
LOUISE:	No, Madame.
COUNTESS:	Then you've clearly never visited Versailles.
	(LAIDRONETTE STOPS RUNNING AND STARTS TO GATHER HER BREATH)
COUNTESS:	The Princess found herself at length on the seashore.
	(THE POLYMNIE MUSIC FROM *LES BOREADES* STARTS TO PLAY AGAIN. OVER THE SEA TOWARDS THE PRINCESS COMES A SMALL GLITTERING BOAT)
COUNTESS:	And there – suddenly - gliding towards her – was a small gilt barque with a sail made of gold brocade and a mast of cedar.
LAIDRONETTE:	But it's beautiful! I have to see!
	(SHE STEPS ON BOARD.)

COUNTESS:	But - as she inspected its treasures - the barque drifted out to sea again. And then suddenly the wind rose and the waves became high.
	(THUNDER AND LIGHTNING. STORM MUSIC. THE BARQUE IS TOSSED UPON A STORMY SEA.)
LAIDRONETTE:	Magotine, Magotine! Is this another of your tricks? If I do die, what does it matter to you or anyone?
	(OUT OF THE STORMY SEA THE GREEN SERPENT EMERGES COIL AFTER COIL.)
SERPENT:	Princess! Princess! I will save you. Trust me, princess, I will save you.
LAIDRONETTE:	No!
	(THE SERPENT'S GREEN COILS WRAP AROUND LAIDRONETTE'S BODY.)
SERPENT:	Without me, you will drown.
LAIDRONETTE:	(PANICKING) No! No! Let me alone! I'd rather drown. I don't want to owe my life to you. You frighten me – you monster!
	(BUT THE COILS REMAIN WRAPPED AROUND HER BODY.)
LAIDRONETTE:	(CRYING OUT) Stop! What are you doing?
SERPENT:	Taking you to safety.
LAIDRONETTE:	Let go at once-
SERPENT:	But princess-
LAIDRONETTE:	Let go I say-
SERPENT:	(SADLY) Ah princess, if you knew me better, you'd fear me less.
	(THE COILS UNWRAP FROM HER BODY. THE STORM ABATES.)
COUNTESS:	And with those words, the serpent plunged beneath the surf. But Laidronette by then was safely on the shore.
LOUISE:	Madame, this coiled snake –
COUNTESS:	It disturbs you?
LOUISE:	(RELUCTANTLY) Yes.
COUNTESS:	Talk to that wonderful husband of yours. (PAUSE) Meanwhile, thanks to the serpent, Laidronette was safely on shore. But her adventures were not over.
	(TINY FIGURES LIKE ORIENTAL POTTERY FIGURES WITH NODDING HEADS APPEAR. TO ACCOMPANY

(THEM - THE AIR OF THE PAGODS FROM RAMEAU'S *LES PALADINS*.)
(A TINY ORIENTAL FIGURE EMERGES TO GREET THE PRINCESS.)

PAGOD: All hail, all hail the princess.
LAIDRONETTE: I don't understand.
PAGOD: We are pagods, grotesque to contemplate, I know, but we are the willing subjects of the ruler of this land. We have been commanded to do our utmost to serve you. I am the Chief Pagod at your service. Follow me if you would be so gracious.
LAIDRONETTE: (FOLLOWING) Where are you taking me?
PAGOD: To a pavilion of green and gold brocade. Within are two baths of crystal filled with deliciously scented water.
LAIDRONETTE: (RELIEVED) Ahh!

(LAIDRONETTE ENTERS THE BATH PREPARED FOR HER. A SENSUOUS THRILL. THEN A MOMENT OF PANIC.)

LAIDRONETTE: But there are two baths.
PAGOD: One is for you, the other for the King of the pagods.
LAIDRONETTE: Your King! But where is he?
PAGOD: Madam, he is presently with the army waging war against his enemies. You will see him as soon as he returns.
LAIDRONETTE: Your King – is he married?
PAGOD: No, madam. Our King is so charming that he has yet to find anyone who would be worthy of him.

(LAIDRONETTE REMAINS CAUGHT IN CONFUSION AS THE LIGHTS FADE.)

COUNTESS: The pagods dressed her in beautiful clothes and waited on her hand and foot. They brought her books to read, food to eat and instruments to play. The days passed in revelry and dancing. But somehow, awake at night in her bed, Laidronette knew all this was not quite enough.

(LAIDRONETTE LIES IN DIMMED LIGHTING UNDER AN EXQUISITE COUNTERPANE, ILL AT EASE.)

LAIDRONETTE: What is to become of me? I can't remain here forever. My days are more pleasant than I could have dared hope. Nobody mocks my looks or runs from me in disgust. And yet – my heart tells me there's something missing.

(A VOICE SPEAKS IN THE DARKNESS BEHIND HER.)

VOICE: Ah, Princess –
LAIDRONETTE: (SCARED) Who's there?

VOICE:	You wouldn't feel so empty if you were prepared to open your heart – and fall in love.
LAIDRONETTE:	Who is this? Are you one of the pagods?
VOICE:	Oh no.
LAIDRONETTE:	Then - who are you?
VOICE:	(SLOWLY) I am the unhappy ruler of this realm, madam.
LAIDRONETTE:	The King! But why are you unhappy?
VOICE:	Because - I adore you. I can't even speak to you without trembling.
LAIDRONETTE:	But how can you possibly adore me? Are you a King with eyes?
VOICE:	Oh yes.
LAIDRONETTE:	Then you must know that I am the ugliest person in the world.
VOICE:	Oh, I have seen you, madam, and know you are not what you think yourself to be. Whether it's for your person, your merit or your misfortunes, I don't know – but I repeat: I adore you.
LAIDRONETTE:	You cannot!
VOICE:	Only my feelings of respect and timidity oblige me to keep myself hidden.
LAIDRONETTE:	Then I'm grateful to you for that. (MORE AGITATED:) But how could I possibly ever love anyone? What would happen to me?
VOICE:	You will never know if you don't open your heart. (PAUSE) But I'm upsetting you. Do you want me to go?
LAIDRONETTE:	Yes. It's best if you do.
VOICE:	Are you so afraid of love?
LAIDRONETTE:	If you knew my history then you know I have every reason to fear it. Nobody could truly love somebody as hideous as me.
VOICE:	I love you.
LAIDRONETTE:	Then you must have very strange tastes.
VOICE:	Perhaps - but I have my reasons and if you knew them you would pity me.
LAIDRONETTE:	Tell me what they are.
VOICE:	Alas, I cannot. I cannot.

(A HEARTFELT SIGH AND THE LIGHTS SNAP OFF.)

COUNTESS:	The voice faded away but still it returned night after night and Laidronette soon found only her invisible lover had the power to please her.

(THE COUNTESS LOOKS SHREWDLY AT LOUISE.)

COUNTESS:	Tell me, Louise, have you ever sat in the dark listening to a man pouring out his heart to you?
LOUISE:	(STIFFLY) I have only listened to my husband.
COUNTESS:	You're quite sure about that?
LOUISE:	Madame, do you doubt me?
COUNTESS:	My dear, how could I? You'll just have to use your imagination to picture how compelling Laidronette found the voice of her

invisible suitor. Particularly one night when she awoke to find tears falling on her person.

(AGAIN THE PRINCESS LIES UNDER THE EMBRODIERED COVER IN THE SEMI-DARKNESS.)

VOICE:	(TEARFULLY) Is there really no hope for me?
LAIDRONETTE:	What do you expect of me? How can I love you without knowing or seeing you?
VOICE:	Alas, why make conditions that thwart my desire to please you? The same wicked Magotine who's treated you so badly has condemned me to suffer for seven years.
LAIDRONETTE:	(INTAKE OF BREATH) Magotine has condemned you!
VOICE:	Oh yes. Five years have already elapsed. There are two remaining. I cannot tell you how much it would relieve the bitterness of my suffering if I became your husband.
LAIDRONETTE:	(SLOWLY) You really want me to marry you?
VOICE:	More than anything.
LAIDRONETTE:	I – I don't know what to say.
VOICE:	You said you felt your life was empty.
LAIDRONETTE:	Yes.
VOICE:	You said you never expected to know what it was to be loved.
LAIDRONETTE:	Yes, but –
VOICE:	So will you agree?
LAIDRONETTE:	(VERY QUIETLY) Yes, I will.
VOICE:	You make me the happiest of beings, Laidronette.
LAIDRONETTE:	I am glad.
VOICE:	But there is one request I must make of you. It is extremely important both for you and for me. You must not attempt to look upon me until the full term of my penance has expired.
LAIDRONETTE:	You expect me to wait for two-
VOICE:	Listen – if you are imprudent and succumb to your curiosity, then I shall have to begin serving my sentence all over again. Worse - you will share in my suffering.
LAIDRONETTE:	And if I agree to your request?
VOICE:	Then in time you will find in me all that your heart desires. And you yourself will regain the marvellous beauty Magotine took from you at birth. (PAUSE) Will you agree – for both our sakes?
LAIDRONETTE:	(WARMLY) Oh yes, my love, of course.

(THE LIGHTS SNAP OFF. THE BARQUE OF THE PAGODS TAKES TO THE SEA AGAIN – TO RAMEAU'S MUSIC.)

COUNTESS:	A ship manned by pagods and loaded with presents was sent with letters from Laidronette to her mother, imploring her to come and visit her daughter in her realm. And impelled by a mixture of motherly concern and plain curiosity, the Queen came. She was duly impressed by Laidronette's new splendour

and desperate to find out what this husband who was prepared to marry her still hideous daughter could possibly be like.

(THE QUEEN TALKS WITH LAIDRONETTE.)

QUEEN: My dear, I'm more than a little puzzled. How long is it now that I've been enjoying your magnificent hospitality?
LAIDRONETTE: (DREADING WHAT'S COMING) Seven days, mother.
QUEEN: Seven days! And yet I've still to set eyes on my future son-in-law.
LAIDRONETTE: I've told you, mother. He's out hunting.
QUEEN: Oh, he's out hunting, is he? Well, yesterday he was ill and the day before that he was out fishing and the day before that he was with the army and the day before that you claimed he was on a pilgrimage. What exactly is going on?
LAIDRONETTE: He – he's very shy.
QUEEN: Laidronette, my dear, listen to me. I must be frank and say I think it a little odd that the King should be interested in someone, however loveable in other ways, with such unfortunate looks. Is there something wrong with him too? (PAUSE) You can tell your mother.
LAIDRONETTE: (FINALLY) I - I don't know.
QUEEN: Whatever do you mean?
LAIDRONETTE: I've never seen him.
QUEEN: What!!!
LAIDRONETTE: I've never seen him. But there's a good reason for that. He has only two more years to spend in this state of penance and at the end of that time I shall not only be able to see him but I shall also become beautiful again myself.
QUEEN: You poor deluded child!
LAIDRONETTE: I don't understand.
QUEEN: Don't you see? You're walking into a trap. How could you have been so naïve as to believe such tales?
LAIDRONETTE: But – you haven't –
QUEEN: Laidronette, listen to your mother. There's only one reason why this husband of yours hides away – he's a hideous monster.
LAIDRONETTE: No!
QUEEN: Look at these servants of his – little shrivelled freaks –they're not natural. Like subjects, like ruler.
LAIDRONETTE: But he has such a gentle voice.
QUEEN: All the better to deceive you. If he's got nothing to hide, why is he hiding away?
LAIDRONETTE: But the curse –
QUEEN: You've only his word for all that nonsense. I don't know how you can live with the knowledge that your husband to be is a vile monster.
LAIDRONETTE: He isn't!
QUEEN: Then let him prove it to you.
LAIDRONETTE: No –

QUEEN: I can tell you're wracked with uncertainty. It's only natural. You're never going to feel safe with him until you've cleared up the matter once and for all.

(THE LIGHTS SNAP OFF.)

COUNTESS: Well, of course, Laidronette resisted her mother's advice as best she could. But the thoughts her mother had brought to the surface wouldn't leave her. We all know how powerful mothers can be.

(LAIDRONETTE AGAIN LIES UNDER THE EXQUISITE COUNTERPANE LISTENING TO HER LOVER.)

VOICE: (SOFTLY) Soon we will be married, Laidronette. How I long for that moment.
LAIDRONETTE: If only-
VOICE: If only what?
LAIDRONETTE: Forgive me – but I have to –
VOICE: Have to?
LAIDRONETTE: I cannot remain in doubt.

(SHE PICKS UP A LAMP. THE LIGHT ILLUMINATES THE BEDROOM. THE GREEN SERPENT IS REVEALED, HIS COILS WRITHING. LAIDRONETTE GIVES A SCREAM.

LAIDRONETTE: Oh no!
VOICE: Cruel woman! Is this my reward?

(THE FIGURE OF THE FAIRY MAGOTINE EMERGES FROM THE DARKNESS AND STANDS THERE CACKLING TRIUMPHANTLY.)

LAIDRONETTE: (AGHAST) What have I done?
VOICE: You have destroyed us.
LAIDRONETTE: If I could only undo what I have done!
MAGOTINE: (SWEEPING IN) But you cannot. My curse still falls – on both of you.

(SHE POSES TRIUMPHANTLY OVER THE TWO LOVERS. SUDDENLY THE LIGHT FADES AS LOUISE SPEAKS.)

LOUISE: But - Madame-
COUNTESS: What is it, my dear?
LOUISE: Surely this cannot be the end. Laidronette cannot be left to suffer in this way.
COUNTESS: My dear, if you imagine this is the end, then you must have an even bleaker view of human existence than I do.

LOUISE: But how can she possibly-
COUNTESS: Of course, in my story, love is redeemed – but only after a number of trials set by the Fairy Magotine.

(MAGOTINE ABOVE A TOILING LAIDRONETTE.)

MAGOTINE: Take these spiders' webs and make me a net strong enough to catch salmon with.
LAIDRONETTE: But the web's barely strong enough to catch flies.
MAGOTINE: Do as I say!

(A NEW COMMAND:)

MAGOTINE: Put this millstone round your neck. Climb to the top of that mountain that soars above the sky. There – gather enough four-leaf clovers to fill a basket-
LAIDRONETTE: But the millstone is ten times heavier than I am.
MAGOTINE: That's your problem. If you don't do as I order, then your precious green serpent will suffer.

(A FINAL ORDER:)

MAGOTINE: Put on these heavy iron shoes. I want you to go down into the underworld and demand the essence of long life from Queen Proserpine. I'm afraid of falling ill and perhaps dying.
LAIDRONETTE: Will you never tire of persecuting me?
MAGOTINE: If you want to save that serpent lover of yours, you'd better get going.
LAIDRONETTE: (DESPERATELY) I cannot... I cannot... (A SUDDEN EFFORT) But I will...

(LIGHTS FADE ON THE EXHAUSTED PRINCESS.)

LOUISE: And did the Princess Laidronette perform these impossible tasks?
COUNTESS: Oh yes.
LOUISE: But how?
COUNTESS: With the help of her love for the King – and her Fairy Protectrice.
LOUISE: Who was she?
COUNTESS: A good fairy who gave her help and good advice.
LOUISE: You haven't mentioned her before.
COUNTESS: She wasn't needed in the story before. By her brave attitude, the Princess made her own luck. And so in time after all her terrible trials the Princess Laidronette became both wise and beautiful.
LOUISE: Because she had opened her heart - and did these terrible things because she loved the green serpent?
COUNTESS: Just so. You understand very well – for a respectable married lady.

LOUISE:	And the Fairy Magotine?
COUNTESS:	In the end even Magotine could not resist the power of love.

(THE GOOD FAIRIES FLUTTER ABOVE AS LAIDRONETTE EMBRACES THE WRITHING GREEN SERPENT. RETURN OF THE POLHYMNIE MUSIC)

COUNTESS:	And the serpent? well, when the time of Laidronette's travails were over and she had bravely and devotedly completed all her tasks, the curse was lifted and he turned into a most beautiful young man –

(THE SERPENT SHEDS ITS COILS AND BECOMES A BEAUTIFUL YOUNG MAN.)

SERPENT KING:	My lovely princess-
LAIDRONETTE:	My handsome king-
SERPENT KING:	Your love has redeemed me.
LAIDRONETTE:	Your love has made me beautiful.
SERPENT KING:	Embrace me, my love.

(THEY EMBRACE. JUST AS THE EMBRACING GETS PASSIONATE, LIGHTS AND MUSIC SNAP OFF.)
(THE COUNTESS TURNS IN HER CHAIR AND SMILES AT LOUISE, WHO LOOKS TROUBLED.)

COUNTESS:	Thus ends the tale of the green serpent.
LOUISE:	(HESITANTLY) Madame, forgive me-
COUNTESS:	Didn't you like my tale?
LOUISE:	Oh yes - but you have a reason for selecting this particular story-
COUNTESS:	Is that how it seems to you?
LOUISE:	I – I don't know.
COUNTESS:	The story undoubtedly demonstrates the power of love.
LOUISE:	Yes, but-
COUNTESS:	But what?
LOUISE:	There's more. The princess could not bear not to know. She – she insisted on knowing what the prince was really like – even though it nearly destroyed her.
COUNTESS:	You mean her curiosity was almost fatal?
LOUISE:	Yes, in a way, but-
COUNTESS:	It was also very natural.
LOUISE:	Yes. (PAUSE) In the circumstances, I think I would be tempted to act like her.
COUNTESS:	You'd want to throw light into corners where light is best not shed?
LOUISE:	I suppose that is what I mean, yes.
COUNTESS:	Best to know if your husband really is a monster you mean.

(AN UNCOMFORTABLE PAUSE)

LOUISE:	Madame, I see I was right. You were seeking to trap me.
COUNTESS:	Trap you! Whatever do you mean?
LOUISE:	You want me to tell you the truth about my husband.
COUNTESS:	My dear, you told me how happy you are with him.
LOUISE:	You know I wasn't telling the truth.
COUNTESS:	My dear, I know no such thing. (PAUSE) Is he so very monstrous?
LOUISE:	(FINALLY) Yes.
COUNTESS:	And he can't be changed however much you try to love him?
LOUISE:	He cares only for the money I brought with me.
COUNTESS:	And your loving parents gave you a choice between this rich marriage and the convent?
LOUISE:	Yes.
COUNTESS:	Does he hit you?
LOUISE:	No. Mostly he is indifferent to me. But he criticises me for my stupidity and lack of beauty. He boasts to me of the whores he visits when he is in Paris and – and of the bed tricks they perform for him. I have tried to make him love me but he just laughs at me. Sometimes I am so upset that I –

(HER VOICE FALTERS INTO SILENCE.

COUNTESS:	(CALMLY) My dear, every young woman wishes her husband dead at some point or other. It's perfectly normal.
LOUISE:	But I don't wish him dead.
COUNTESS:	Don't you? (PAUSE) There's still time to tell you how close I came to getting my husband executed.
LOUISE:	(SCARED) No, no
COUNTESS:	You see, after two years of hateful marriage, I was sickened by his meanness, his joyless love-making, his brutality, his chasing after page boys, his stupidity, his snobbery - and I thought I would run mad if I wasn't free of him.
LOUISE:	I don't want to hear.
COUNTESS:	I think you do. In despair, I went to my mother, a widow then and living openly with her aristocratic lover. So we all put our heads together – along with my lover, of course.
LOUISE:	No, no –
COUNTESS:	We devised a plot to kill my husband. You know the punishment for openly criticising the King? The Count d'Aulnoy hated paying his taxes. He was congenitally mean and hopelessly disorganised but that didn't stop him blaming the King for all his problems. If we could only get witnesses then he would be accused of lese majesté and executed.
LOUISE:	Madame, forgive me-
COUNTESS:	Why?
LOUISE:	I must go. I'm not feeling well. In any case, I've already overstayed my welcome.
COUNTESS:	This is very sudden.
LOUISE:	I should not have said what I said.

COUNTESS:	I shall not repeat it.
LOUISE:	All the same, it's best if it was as if it had not been said.
COUNTESS:	You are my guest and may say what you like.
LOUISE:	No, Madame, I may not. If you will excuse me-
COUNTESS:	I will not force you to stay.
LOUISE:	You have been most hospitable, Madame. The fault is all mine.
COUNTESS:	Don't blame yourself. You only listened.
LOUISE:	I am not well.

(SUDDENLY SHE RISES FROM HER SEAT, FIGHTING BACK TEARS.)

LOUISE:	Goodbye, Madame, and thank you.
COUNTESS:	Please call again.
LOUISE:	Thank you, Madame, but it's best if I do not. Goodbye.

(SHE BURSTS INTO TEARS AND RUNS OUT OF THE GARDEN.)
(A PAUSE. THE COUNTESS GIVES A SIGH.)

COUNTESS: (WITH A SIGH) So much for wishes.

(THE LIGHTS FADE TO DARKNESS.)

PART TWO

(ANOTHER DAY IN THE GARDEN.)
(THE COUNTESS IS WRITING A LETTER.)
(THE COWS MOO. THE COUNTESS TURNS TO THEM WEARILY.)

COUNTESS: Moo! Mooooo! Mooooo! Moooooo!

(SHE SIGHS AND RETURNS TO HER LETTER.)
(THE STEWARD ENTERS.)

COUNTESS: The black horse?
STEWARD: Has recovered from its sprained fetlock.
COUNTESS: So can we take a drive?
STEWARD: Unfortunately not, my lady. The grey horse –
COUNTESS: Is sulking? Has had a temper tantrum?
STEWARD: No, my lady, it's lame.
COUNTESS: Something to do with ploughing, I suppose.
STEWARD: Indeed, my lady. It is likely to recover –
COUNTESS: But not for quite a few weeks.
STEWARD: You understand these matters, my lady.

(HE BOWS AND LEAVES. THE COUNTESS GIVES A SIGH THEN STARTS TO READ HER LETTER OVER.)

COUNTESS: My dear Eloise, it is horrible to think that poor Angelique is condemned. I thought she had every chance of proving her innocence if I was not around but it seems everything has conspired against her. A huge injustice is about to be committed. If only the King would –

(SHE STOPS HERSELF AND SCRIBBLES OVER THE PASSAGE WITH HER QUILL PEN.)

COUNTESS: I cannot say that, I must not. Too many lives at stake, not just my own, and every letter likely to be read. (SHE STARTS TO WRITE AGAIN.) My dear Eloise, my thoughts are much with you and other dear friends at this time. Here in my rustic retreat, I have perhaps over ample time to think and –

(THE GARDEN AGAIN STARTS TO RIPPLE MYSTERIOUSLY. THE COUNTESS LOOKS UP.)
(LOUISE HAS SILENTLY ENTERED THE GARDEN.)

LOUISE: Madame, forgive me for intruding in this way. But I owe you an apology.

COUNTESS:	Consider it already accepted.
LOUISE:	But I behaved badly and-
COUNTESS:	Life is really too short to be wasted on things that really don't matter.
LOUISE:	I have been thinking about what you said.
COUNTESS:	I simply told you a story.
LOUISE:	No. There was more in it than that. There was also a second story about – about your husband - and I would not let you finish it. I have no right to intrude upon painful episodes in your life I know but-.
COUNTESS:	But you would like to hear the end?
LOUISE:	Yes. If you're prepared to-
COUNTESS:	Oh yes, I'm prepared. I discovered many years ago that a little pain drains out of something that hurt us each time we tell it over again.

(NEVERTHELESS SHE PAUSES BEFORE SHE SPEAKS.)

COUNTESS:	We should perhaps call this a tale on the vanity of human wishes. At the time I did think myself not responsible. I thought it only right that my elders should save me from a situation of their rather than my making. It took years for me to see how far it was my will, my need that drove events on. (PAUSE. A SUDDEN TREMOR OF VULNERABILITY) At the end of it, there were two men tortured and executed and neither of them my husband.
LOUISE:	But I don't understand.
COUNTESS:	In this tale everything went wrong. And the suffering is all too real. (PAUSE) My husband turned the tables on us. Here were my mother's lover, the Marquis of Corboyer, and my admirer, the Chevalier de Bonenfant and a well-intentioned gentleman called Lamoiziere all prepared to swear D'Aulnoy had spoken treason to them. Here was D'Aulnoy, an unpopular man at the best of times, immediately arrested and thrown into prison. But he held his nerve. He asked – why would I speak treason aloud to two men I have never met before - to whom I had only just been introduced by the Marquis of Corboyer? It makes no sense. So the three men were called in and questioned together and individually and they contradicted each other and Lamoiziere fell apart and confessed. And that was the end of it. Apart from the torture and execution that is.

(A PAINFUL PAUSE.)

LOUISE:	Did you truly love the Chevalier de Bonenfant, Madame?
COUNTESS:	I can't really remember. (PAUSE) And, of course, of his screaming and cursing under torture I only heard.
LOUISE:	Oh, Madame-
COUNTESS:	What is it?
LOUISE:	I feel so very sorry for you

COUNTESS:	Don't be. It is over thirty years ago.
LOUISE:	And your mother?
COUNTESS:	She fled to Spain. She's still there. I have visited her once or twice but she's never really forgiven me. You see, she blamed me. It was all done for my benefit and yet it was the man she loved more than any other, her dignified, urbane, grey-haired companion, who died in hideous pain screaming obscenities.
LOUISE:	But it was she who concocted the plan?
COUNTESS:	Oh yes. (PAUSE) I sometimes think that if I had been older and more in charge, I would have planned it better. I know how to plan and tell stories, you see. Or maybe after that grim initiation, I have forced myself to learn.
LOUISE:	I can't imagine surviving something like that.
COUNTESS:	Neither could I at the time. I thought I would be executed too. But I played the innocent young ingenue well enough and they put me into a convent. Quite a fashionable convent. The sisters saw more cavaliers than most women who live at large. In the end, I was allowed to leave the country.
LOUISE:	Where did you go?
COUNTESS:	Spain, England, Italy. I paid my way by the information I picked up and sent back to the French government. I was rather an accomplished spy so eventually I was rewarded for my services by being allowed to return. (BRISKLY) But enough of me. How are your own plans?
LOUISE:	(PUZZLED) Madame?
COUNTESS:	For murdering your husband, I mean.
LOUISE:	Madame, I have no such intention.
COUNTESS:	But I am right in assuming that you do want him dead?
LOUISE:	I do not wish him dead. I only-
COUNTESS:	Wish him not alive and not your husband?

(ANOTHER PAINFUL PAUSE.)

LOUISE:	Madame, I see I cannot deceive you. My father made me marry him. He came to visit us with his bad breath and his lecherous eye and his horrible laugh and – I never imagined my father would insist.
COUNTESS:	And your mother?
LOUISE:	She insisted too.
COUNTESS:	You know something, my dear. I have seen it in your eyes.
LOUISE:	Seen what, Madame?
COUNTESS:	You are in love with someone. Someone else I mean.
LOUISE:	Madame!
COUNTESS:	You're blushing.
LOUISE:	I don't know what you mean, Madame.
COUNTESS:	Well, he's certainly not your husband that's for sure.
LOUISE:	Madame –
COUNTESS:	Yes?
LOUISE:	I would very much like to hear another fairy story.
COUNTESS:	You want to change the subject?

LOUISE:	I'd like to hear another tale.
COUNTESS:	That is not necessarily the same thing. But I am delighted to oblige you, my dear.

(THE FANFARE AGAIN RINGS OUT. THE GARDEN SHIMMERS BACK INTO DARKNESS LEAVING THE COUNTESS AND LOUISE IN LIGHT.)

COUNTESS:	I call this the Tale of the Yellow Dwarf and the King of the Golden Mines. Once upon a time there was a Queen. Now the queen was a widow and she had only one daughter –

(COURTLY DANCE MUSIC – BY RAMEAU)
(LIGHTS. THE QUEEN WATCHES AS HER DAUGHTER – TOUTEBELLE – DANCES AT A BALL.)

QUEEN:	Come to me, Toutbelle, you've danced enough.
TOUTEBELLE:	But I'm enjoying myself.
QUEEN:	You'll tire yourself out.
TOUTEBELLE:	Of course, I won't. And every man in the room wants a dance with me.
QUEEN:	I really think you should stop.
TOUTEBELLE:	Don't be silly, maman. I can't disappoint my admirers now can I?
QUEEN:	(WITH A SIGH.) Oh very well.
TOUTEBELLE:	Thank you, maman.

(SHE DANCES OFF TRIUMPHANTLY.)

COUNTESS:	The fact was that the Queen was so afraid of losing her daughter's affection that she never corrected any of her faults. To cap it all, she had fuelled her daughter's vanity by naming her Toutebelle. Nevertheless, twenty neighbouring kings still vied to marry her.

(THREE KINGS ON THEIR KNEES BEFORE TOUTEBELLE.)

FIRST KING:	Mercy, fair princess –
SECOND KING:	I long to be with you–
THIRD KING:	I worship the very ground you tread on.
ALL KINGS:	(AS ONE) Ah, princess, ahhhhh…

(TOUTEBELLE YAWNS AND WANDERS OFF.)

COUNTESS:	Unfortunately, a man might have hanged himself five or six times a day to please her and the Princess Toutebelle would have thought it but a trifle. So a deputation of Kings complained to the Queen.

(THE KINGS KNEEL BEFORE THE QUEEN.)

FIRST KING:	We cannot endure this waiting –
SECOND KING:	She keeps us all on tenterhooks –
THIRD KING:	She must choose one of us to end this agony.
ALL KINGS:	(AS ONE) Help us, please…
QUEEN:	I only wish I could.
FIRST KING;	But you are her mother –
SECOND KING:	You are responsible –
THIRD KING:	You made her this way –
ALL KINGS:	(AS ONE) Help us, please…
QUEEN:	It is beneath my royal dignity to admit, your majesties, but I think you have a point. Something must be done. But what?

(THE QUEEN AND THE THREE KINGS VANISH.)

LOUISE:	(BREAKING IN) Madame-
COUNTESS:	Yes, my dear?
LOUISE:	Is this a reproach to me?
COUNTESS:	Whatever do you mean?
LOUISE:	I obeyed my parents and married. The Princess disobeyed and-
COUNTESS:	(GENTLY) My dear, the tale is only just begun.

(A DESERT SAND STORM. IT SUBSIDES TO SHOW THE QUEEN EDGING HER WAY PAINFULLY ACROSS THE DESERT.)

QUEEN:	Oh this heat, this terrible heat…
COUNTESS:	The Queen decided that her only hope was to consult a famous fairy called the Fairy of the Desert, who was believed to be an expert in such matters. Unfortunately the Desert Fairy lived in the desert and so the Queen's visit to see her was arduous – and dangerous.

(THE QUEEN STARTS TO FALTER.)

QUEEN:	I – I'm going to faint- Ahhh!

(SHE SCREAMS. AHEAD OF HER LIE A HUNGRY PRIDE OF DESERT LIONS.)

QUEEN:	Alas, what will become of me? They're going to devour me. What can I do?

(SOMEONE CLEARS HIS THROAT LOUDLY. THE QUEEN LOOKS ROUND IN PUZZLEMENT. ANOTHER THROAT CLEAR. THE QUEEN IS STILL PUZZLED)

DWARF:	Ahem – excuse me, your majesty.

(THE YELLOW DWARF SITS IN A TREE JUST ABOVE HER EATING AN ORANGE.)

DWARF: I see you're afraid, your majesty.
QUEEN: I fear the lions will eat me.
DWARF: More than likely. They've eaten plenty of others before you.
QUEEN: Then I must prepare to die. And it's all my daughter's fault.
DWARF: You have a daughter?
QUEEN: Yes.
DWARF: That's interesting. I've been looking for a wife for some time.
QUEEN: Yes, but-
DWARF: Please yourself. If you promise me your daughter in marriage, I'll save you from the lions. But I wouldn't hesitate too long if I were you.

(THE LIONS ROAR. THE QUEEN HESITATES.)

COUNTESS: It was not an easy decision. The dwarf was not only very short but also very ugly and very, very yellow all over. On the other hand the lions had two heads each and four rows of terrifyingly sharp teeth.
DWARF: Well? Make your mind up.
QUEEN: (FINALLY) My lord dwarf, Toutebelle is yours.
DWARF: I'm not sure I want her.
QUEEN: (DESPERATELY) But she is the loveliest princess in the world.
DWARF: Oh very well then. I'll accept her as my wife out of charity. But don't forget what you've promised me.

(A HUGE CLAP OF THUNDER. THE LIGHTS FADE ON THE DWARF AND THE LIONS.)
(LIGHTS UP ON THE QUEEN LYING UNDER HER COVERLET MOANING IN A DELIRIUM.)

QUEEN: No, no, save me… (PAUSE) Where am I?
TOUTEBELLE: (GENTLY) You're here in the palace, maman. You've been in a fever for days.
QUEEN: (URGENTLY) Toutebelle-
TOUTEBELLE: Yes, maman.
QUEEN: I – I'm still a little confused but – I want you to promise me something.
TOUTEBELLE: Of course, maman.
QUEEN: None of your tricks now.
TOUTEBELLE: Oh, maman, I'm so pleased to see you better. Of course, I promise.
QUEEN: Then – please – get married as soon as possible.
TOUTEBELLE: Get married! But whom shall I choose?
QUEEN: Whoever you like most. You have my blessing. But – please – get married.
TOUTEBELLE: I promise.

QUEEN:	Do you know which King you will choose?
TOUTEBELLE:	(QUIETLY) Oh yes.
QUEEN:	So which King is it?
TOUTEBELLE:	The King of the Golden Mines. (PAUSE) He is the handsomest of the Kings by far. He's also very, very rich.
QUEEN:	Could you not have chosen him before?
TOUTEBELLE:	But, maman, I had the devotion of twenty kings. Why should I rush to choose one of them?
QUEEN:	(WEARILY) Why indeed?
	<u>WEDDING MUSIC, COURTESY OF RAMEAU. A WEDDING PROCESSION LEAD BY TOUTEBELLE AND THE KING OF THE GOLDEN MINES WHO GRACIOUSLY ACKNOWLEDGE THE CHEERS.)</u>
COUNTESS:	Strange to say, the Princess had chosen very well. The King was not only handsome, he was also brave and clever. The people loved him – not least because he ordered great sacks of gold coins to be brought from his mines and distributed to them. The happy couple entered the church accompanied by the cheering of the crowds.
	<u>(THE MUSIC FADES. AS THE PROCESSION APPROACHES THE CHURCH, A LARGE BOX ON WHEELS DRAWN BY TWO TURKEY COCKS APPEARS – ACCOMPANIED BY THE AGED AND UGLY DESERT FAIRY.)</u>
DESERT FAIRY:	Stop! Stop at once!
QUEEN:	Excuse me – who are you?
DESERT FAIRY:	Don't you know? I'm the Desert Fairy.
QUEEN:	(MAKING THE BEST OF IT) Greetings, Desert Fairy. We welcome you to-
DESERT FAIRY:	(CUTTING IN) Do you think you can break your promises to my friend, the Yellow Dwarf, with impunity? If it hadn't been for him, you would have been devoured by lions.
QUEEN:	I appreciate that but-
DESERT FAIRY:	We do not put up with such insults in fairyland! Your daughter is promised to the dwarf!
QUEEN:	But-
TOUTEBELLE:	Maman, what is she saying?
	<u>(THE KING ADVANCES TOWARDS THE DESERT FAIRY, SWORD IN HAND.)</u>
KING:	Enough, old woman! I am the King of the Golden Mines and I am about to be married to the Princess Toutebelle.
DESERT FAIRY:	Don't try to threaten me. I'm only telling the truth.
KING:	I said – enough! Leave this palace for ever – or else!
DESERT FAIRY:	You'll regret this!

(A HUGE BOING!!! EFFECT. THE BOX BURSTS OPEN AND OUT OF IT SPRINGS THE YELLOW DWARF MOUNTED ON A HUGE TOM CAT.)

DWARF: Not so fast, young man.
KING: Out of my way!
DWARF: Don't think you can assault this illustrious fairy. You're going to have to deal with me first.
KING: Who are you?
DWARF: I'm your foe. No, worse, I'm your rival. The princess Toutebelle is promised to me.
KING: Miserable midget! You have the audacity to declare yourself the lover of this divine princess?
DWARF: I do as a matter of fact.
KING: How dare you! I would long since have eliminated you if you had really been worthy of dying by my hand.
DWARF: Is that so?

(THE DWARF ON HIS CAT LEAPS AT THE KING.)

KING: Have at you, dwarf!
DWARF: Have at you!

(THEY START TO FIGHT. THE LIGHTING GROWS RED AND THEN FADES INTO SEMI-DARKNESS. THE FIGURES ARE BARELY VISIBLE.)

COUNTESS: The sun suddenly became as red as blood and it grew so dark they could scarcely see each other. The King fought bravely. But then the Desert Fairy rushed towards the Princess – and stabbed her.

(IN THE CONFUSION AND DARKNESS, THE PRINCESS CRIES OUT. THE KING RUNS TOWARDS HER. SO DOES THE DWARF. SWIRLING SHADOWS IN THE GLOOM.)

COUNTESS: The King rushed to rescue her. But the Dwarf was quicker. Leaping back on to his tom cat, he snatched the Princess from the arms of the Queen and disappeared with his prize.

(AS THE LIGHTS DIM, THE KING CRIES OUT.)

KING: (IN DESPAIR) Toutebelle! Toutebelle! Come back! Come back! What's happening? What's happening?

(HIS CRIES FADE INTO THE DARKNESS.)

COUNTESS: (CALMLY) Dear me! Love, cruel Love! Is this how you treat two young lovers who acknowledge you as their lord?

LOUISE:	Just when each of them had found an ideal partner. It seems so sad.
COUNTESS:	Don't forget that she was promised to the Yellow Dwarf.
LOUISE:	That was her mother's doing.
COUNTESS:	My dear, you are in love with someone else, aren't you?
LOUISE:	I just hope your story has a happy ending for the young lovers.
COUNTESS:	My dear Louise, I've told you one story with a happy ending. How many more can you reasonably expect? The King awoke to find himself chained to a rock in a gloomy cave.

(LIGHTS UP ON THE KING – CHAINED TO A ROCK IN A GLOOMY CAVE.)

KING: Where am I? Where is Toutebelle? Help me somebody? Can anyone hear me?

(THE DESERT FAIRY APPEARS – DISGUISED AS A BEAUTIFUL YOUNG NYMPH.)

DESERT FAIRY:	(DISGUISED AS NYMPH) I hear you, handsome prince. And I pity your suffering.
COUNTESS:	Perhaps I should explain. The Desert Fairy had no sooner set eyes upon the King than she had become infatuated with him. So now the Desert Fairy made use of her magic powers to appear as a beautiful nymph.
DESERT FAIRY:	So – tell me - why are you chained here?
KING:	Alas, fair nymph, I don't know why but I fear I have been brought here by that cursed Desert Fairy.
DESERT FAIRY:	She wants to marry you. And she's very determined when she sets her mind on something.
KING:	Alas!
DESERT FAIRY:	But if you trust me, I can help you.
KING:	Thank you, fair nymph.

(THE FAIR NYMPH APPROACHES. AS SHE NEARS, THE KING GLANCES DOWN - AND SEES HIDEOUSLY GNARLED GRIFFIN'S FEET.)

COUNTESS: Fortunately for the King, there was one part of her anatomy the Desert Fairy could not change with even her most powerful magic. Her feet. So the King was immediately put on his guard.

KING: (THINKING CAREFULLY) Ah, fair nymph, you must understand that I don't feel any aversion towards the Desert Fairy as such.

DESERT FAIRY: (INTRIGUED) Oh?

KING: It's just that I find it difficult to cope with the fact that she's protected the Yellow Dwarf and chained me up. What have I done to offend her? It's true that I loved a beautiful princess but

	if the Desert Fairy restored my liberty to me, I feel sure that gratitude would lead me to love no one but her.
DESERT FAIRY:	(FLUSTERED) Do you really mean that?
KING:	Of course. I am not experienced in the art of deception. Wouldn't any man's vanity be flattered if he was wooed by a powerful fairy instead of a mere princess? But, of course, it's difficult to feel anything except hatred when I'm chained like this.
DESERT FAIRY:	Things would change if you weren't chained?
KING:	Can you doubt it?
DESERT FAIRY:	Let's see.

(SHE MAKES A GESTURE. THE KING'S CHAINS FALL FROM HIM. LIGHTS FADE.)

COUNTESS:	Meanwhile the Princess Toutebelle languished inside a castle made entirely of steel. Her wounds had healed but what did that matter when her heart still bled?

(INSIDE THE STEEL PALACE THE DWARF APPROACHES TOUTEBELLE.)

DWARF:	Princess-
TOUTEBELLE:	I will not listen.
DWARF:	You've not allowed me to say anything yet.
TOUTEBELLE:	You killed my love. I will not marry you.
DWARF:	Says who? Don't forget your mother promised you to me.
TOUTEBELLE:	Am I bound by my mother's promises?
DWARF:	Frankly – yes. Or would you have preferred to see your mother eaten by lions?
TOUTEBELLE:	Of course not. But I don't love you.
DWARF:	You can learn.
TOUTEBELLE:	Never!
DWARF:	Oh, it'll take less time than that. Perhaps you'd like to look up into the heavens. Tell me what you see?

(THE KING FLOATS BY THROUGH THE ETHER WITH THE DESERT FAIRY STILL IN HER NYMPH DISGUISE.)

TOUTEBELLE:	(HORRIFIED) My love – the King –
DWARF:	Consorting with a beautiful nymph. So he's not as dead as you thought he was.
TOUTEBELLE:	Alas, is there no end to my suffering?
DWARF:	There's always an end if you'll agree to marry me.
TOUTEBELLE:	Never! Even after this – never!

(MEANWHILE THE KING AND THE DISGUISED DESERT FAIRY ARE STILL FLOATING THROUGH THE ETHER.)

DESERT FAIRY:	Did you by any chance look down just now and see the Princess Toutebelle?
KING:	You know I did. She was crying. She was in deep distress.
DESERT FAIRY:	Did it upset you?
KING:	(WITH A BIG EFFORT) Of course it aroused feelings in me. But you are the Desert Fairy and infinitely her superior in mind.
DESERT FAIRY:	You know I am the Desert Fairy?
KING:	Of course. Who could fail to perceive your innate loveliness through this disguise?
DESERT FAIRY:	Have I really inspired you with sentiments so favourable?
KING:	You know you have. All I ask is a token of your good will towards me.
DESERT FAIRY:	And what token is that?
KING:	I hope you will not refuse me when I ask you to protect Toutebelle.
DESERT FAIRY:	Reflect on what you ask of me.
KING:	I know I ask a great deal.
DESERT FAIRY:	You ask too much. The Yellow Dwarf is my best friend. Do you want me to use my skills against him? In order to release a woman I still regard as my rival?
KING:	How can I prove I love you?
DESERT FAIRY:	That's a very good question.
KING:	I only need time.
DESERT FAIRY:	(SUSPICIOUSLY) Time?
KING:	To make myself worthy of you.
DESERT FAIRY:	In what way?
KING:	My appearance – after all these adventures – is not what it might be.
DESERT FAIRY:	You need a scented bath?
KING:	Yes.
DESERT FAIRY:	Fresh clothes?
KING:	Oh yes.
DESERT FAIRY:	Expensive jewellery?
KING:	Oh yes. (PAUSE) If you don't mind.
DESERT FAIRY:	(INFATUATED) Oh no, not at all. (GULP) You are a very beautiful young man.

(LIGHTS FADE ON THE TRANSFORMATION OF THE KING INTO HIS FORMER BEAUTY.)

COUNTESS:	The Desert Fairy became so infatuated with the King that she gave him liberties that her more cautious self would never have allowed. She even gave him permission to walk daily by the seaside. (PAUSE) Older women sometimes have these feelings for lovely young men. (PAUSE) So, of course, do young women now and then.
LOUISE:	(EMBARRASSED) Oh, Madame.

(THE KING WALKS BY THE SEASHORE.)

KING:	Oh Toutebelle, my Toutebelle, how I miss you! Can you hear me, Spirit of the Ocean? If it's true that you protect lovers then rise now from your coral caves and help a despairing lover.

(MAGIC MUSIC – THE ENTRY OF POLYMNIE AGAIN – AS A MERMAID RISES FROM THE SEA.)

MERMAID:	I have heard of your sad predicament. If you trust me, I can rescue you.
KING:	(ENTRANCED) I trust you completely, lovely mermaid. I am at my wits' end and you give me hope out of nowhere.
MERMAID:	I have seen your unhappy princess daily and her beauty and merit have aroused my compassion.
KING:	Please – take me to her.
MERMAID:	I will do as you ask – but there is something you must know.
KING:	What is that?
MERMAID:	The Princess saw you floating through the ether with the Desert Fairy. Except she did not know it was the Desert Fairy. She thought it was a beautiful nymph.
KING:	So she believes I love someone else?
MERMAID:	Consult your own heart.
KING:	What do you mean?
MERMAID:	I am sure you will be able to persuade her of your fidelity.
KING:	I stake my life upon it.
MERMAID:	Then follow me.

(THE MERMAID LEADS THE KING TOWARDS THE PALACE OF STEEL.)

MERMAID:	We are now approaching the castle of steel.

(SHE MAGICS A GLIMMERING SWORD OUT OF THE AIR.)

MERMAID:	Here is a sword fashioned from a single diamond. You will need it to defend yourself against your foes. It will help you brave the greatest dangers.
KING:	Thank you, mermaid, thank you.
MERMAID:	But one word of warning. You must never - ever - let this sword drop from your hand. If you do, you will be in grave danger. Adieu.
KING:	Adieu.

(THE MERMAID SINKS BACK INTO THE SEA.)
(THE KING TURNS HIS ATTENTION TOWARDS THE CASTLE. SUDDENLY A TERRIBLE MONSTER APPEARS. HE FLASHES HIS SWORD AT IT.)
(THE MONSTER SLINKS AWAY WITH A WHIMPER.)

COUNTESS: But then a greater and more confusing challenge presented itself. Three graceful nymphs advanced towards him.

(SEDUCTIVE MUSIC, COURTESY OF RAMEAU. THREE VERY SEDUCTIVE NYMPHS APPEAR.)
(THE KING RAISES HIS SWORD THEN HESITATES.)
(THE MERMAID RISES AGAIN.)

MERMAID: Strike! Strike! Or your princess is lost forever!

(AS THE MERMAID SINKS AGAIN, THE KING ATTACKS THE WOMEN WITH HIS SWORD. THEY SCREAM AND SCATTER IN A CONFUSION OF MOVEMENT AND LIGHT)
(AS THEY SCATTER, TOUTEBELLE IS REVEALED.)
(THE KING MOVES TO EMBRACE HER BUT SHE TURNS ASIDE WITH A REPROACHFUL LOOK.)

TOUTEBELLE: Ah, my King, my dear King, you said you loved me—
KING: That is why I am here.
TOUTEBELLE: But I saw you sailing through the air with a lady of extraordinary beauty.
KING: Please, princess, do not doubt me. It is only you I love. I've come to release you from the Yellow Dwarf.

(HE SINKS TO HIS KNEES IN FRONT OF HER, LAYING ASIDE THE MAGIC SWORD.)

KING: Don't reject the aid of the most faithful of lovers. Please!

(SUDDENLY THE YELLOW DWARF IS THERE. HE HOLDS A DAGGER IN HIS HAND AND ADVANCES TOWARDS THE DEFENCELESS KING.)

DWARF: Good day to your majesty!
TOUTEBELLE: Don't harm him – please.
DWARF: Don't harm him – when he is in my power and wanted to steal you from me, princess?
TOUTEBELLE: Spare him – please.
KING: I am unarmed.
DWARF: Very foolish of you in the circumstances – particularly when you'd been given a powerful magic sword.
KING: I still defy you.
DWARF: Do you? Well, I'll give you a choice. I'll spare your life so long as you let me marry the Princess.
KING: Never!
DWARF: You're sure about that?
KING: I'd rather die.
TOUTEBELLE: Don't say that.
KING: I'd rather die than let you marry this monster.

TOUTEBELLE:	Then let us die together.
KING:	No, Princess, let me die for you.
TOUTEBELLE:	Dwarf, listen – rather than let him die, I agree to marry you.
DWARF:	You'll marry me?
TOUTEBELLE:	Yes.
KING:	I'd rather die than see you married to him.
DWARF:	(COOLLY) Well, that's easily arranged.

(WITH A SUDDEN BRUTAL GESTURE THE DWARF STABS THE KING. THE KING COLLAPSES CLUTCHING HIS WOUND.)

KING: Ahhh…

(FOR A MOMENT HE SUMMONS ALL HIS ENERGY TO REACH TOWARDS THE PRINCESS. BUT HIS STRENGTH GIVES OUT AND HE FALLS BACK DYING.)

TOUTEBELLE: (WEEPING) My love, oh my love, don't die. Please don't die.

(THE KING DIES. THE PRINCESS GIVES OUT A WAIL OF GRIEF.)

TOUTEBELLE: No! No! No! My love, oh my love. Without you, I am… nothing…

(SHE FALLS DEAD BY HIS BODY.)
(THE DWARF STARES COLDLY AT THE TWO BODIES AS THE LIGHTS FADE.)

COUNTESS: The wicked Dwarf much preferred to see the Princess dead than in the arms of his rival. The Desert Fairy, when she learned what had happened, felt very much the same.

(GENTLE MUSIC AS THE MERMAID RISES AGAIN.)

COUNTESS: Only the Mermaid regretted the death of the lovers. But the only favour she could gain from Fate was to turn them into palm trees.

(TWO PALM TREES RISE FROM THE GROUND.)

COUNTESS: The bodies of the Princess and the King, so perfect in life, became two lovely trees. Their branches joined in the embraces they had been denied in life.

(LIGHTS FADE ON THE MERMAID AND THE TREES. THE COUNTESS AND LOUISE ARE ALONE AGAIN.)

COUNTESS: So ends the tale of the Yellow Dwarf.

(THEN SHE REGISTERS THAT LOUISE IS WEEPING.)

LOUISE: Oh, Madame, it is such a sad tale.
COUNTESS: I told you that you couldn't always expect a happy ending.
LOUISE: But the Princess started so badly and learned so much. In the end she and the King loved each other so much.
COUNTESS: In the end was too late.
LOUISE:: Do you think so?
COUNTESS: The Princess's troubles came from a vow that was not kept.
LOUISE: Her mother's vow. Perhaps if she'd married the Dwarf all might have been well.
COUNTESS: If you want a husband who is yellow and one foot tall.
LOUISE: Then you think she should have married the handsome King?
COUNTESS: If she'd made up her mind in the first place. But, of course, she didn't.
LOUISE: She was young. She didn't fully understand what love means. (PAUSE) The punishment seems very harsh.
COUNTESS: Punishments often are.
LOUISE: And the Yellow Dwarf was left alive?
COUNTESS: Just like my husband.
LOUISE: (FAINTLY) And mine.

(A PAUSE. THEN LOUISE BURSTS OUT.)

LOUISE: Oh, Madame, if only I knew what to do. You are so very wise.
COUNTESS: I am just a story-teller.
LOUISE: I have made a vow to love, honour and obey.
COUNTESS: You can't make a vow to love anyone.
LOUISE: Just so. And you can't make a vow not to love anyone either.
COUNTESS: Is he young this admirer?
LOUISE: I cannot tell you.
COUNTESS: What would he do for you? Would he suffer like the King of the Golden Mines?
LOUISE: I would not ask that of him, Madame.
COUNTESS: When I was in Spain, I saw the oddest sight. You know that men of a religious disposition are given during Holy Week to whipping themselves furiously as they process down the streets. Flagellants they are called. When these Flagellants meet a handsome woman, they promptly whip themselves at such a rate that the blood flies all over her. This is considered a particular civility and the lady acknowledges and thanks them for it.
LOUISE: Today you seem determined to tell me horrible things.
COUNTESS: Perhaps that is because one of my best friends is under sentence of death.
LOUISE: (APPALLED) Oh, Madame – forgive me –
COUNTESS: I'm glad that you came. Otherwise I would be alone with my thoughts.
LOUISE: But now I should go?

COUNTESS:	Perhaps you should. I was glad to talk to you. But now- I am suddenly very weary.
LOUISE:	I can understand that, Madame.
COUNTESS:	I should warn you of something before you go.
LOUISE:	Madame?
COUNTESS:	The friend I mentioned. She is accused of conspiring to murder her husband, Tiquet, an eminent politician. Some ruffian took a pot shot at him and when arrested implicated Angelique. There is no other proof and her husband survived the attack.
LOUISE:	But she is under sentence of death?
COUNTESS:	Yes – unless his gracious Majesty chooses to pardon her.
LOUISE:	I trust he will. I shall pray for her.
COUNTESS:	That is good of you, my dear. But I want you to remember – I am known for associating with plots to murder husbands.
LOUISE:	I have no such plan. We have no such plan.
COUNTESS:	We?
LOUISE:	(SHYLY) His name is Philippe.
COUNTESS:	Your lover?
LOUISE:	(FIRMLY) My admirer. We love each other – but not in the sense that we are lovers.
COUNTESS:	Be careful.
LOUISE:	We are careful.
COUNTESS:	I mean – when you make your plans.
LOUISE:	There are no plans.
COUNTESS:	(TOUCHED) That is a good answer. (PAUSE) God bless you both. Be off now.
	(SHE KISSES LOUISE. LOUISE LEAVES.) (THE COUNTESS STANDS ALONE.)
COUNTESS:	Am I turning soft in my old age?
	(THE LIGHTS FADE.)

PART THREE

(ANOTHER DAY IN THE GARDEN.)
(THE COUNTESS PACES THE GARDEN IN A STATE OF DISTRESS.)
(A CACOPHONY OF FARM ANIMALS – SHEEP, CATTLE, GOATS. SHE HOLDS HER EARS AGAINST THE NOISE – THEN SHOUTS OUT.)

COUNTESS: Leave me in peace! Stop – please stop!

(THE CACOPHONY STOPS.)
(THE COUNTESS STARTS ONCE MORE TO GO THROUGH THE LETTER SHE IS COMPOSING IN HER HEAD.)

COUNTESS: I can scarcely put pen to paper, Eloise. All I can think of is Angelique's laughter, her vitality, her honesty. And now her head has been brutally separated from her shoulders. You tell me she was brave. Of course, she was brave. That is no consolation. She assured me she had nothing to do with the planning of Robert's death. She would not lie to me – of all people – would she?

(PAUSE)

COUNTESS: Would she? Of course, theirs was a hateful marriage and she would have been happier without him but – she would not lie to me. The King should have listened to her. The King should have pardoned her. She should not have died beneath the axe like a vile criminal. I hate this society of ours with its knowing, smug little circles, all subservient to an ageing tyrant who screwed around in his youth and now professes piety. Angelique was an honest woman. One of the few. She should not have been executed.

(PAUSE. SHE STOPS AND SHAKES HER HEAD.)

COUNTESS: I cannot send a letter like that.

(SHE PACES THE GARDEN IN AGITATION.)

COUNTESS: There were three daughters – one talked too much, one was very vain and one – no, she wasn't vain, they're always vain. She was lazy. Three daughters of a queen – no, it's always a queen. Three daughters of a King, one who talked too much, one who-

(THE STEWARD ENTERS.)

STEWARD:	My lady, if you desire a drive in a coach through the countryside –
COUNTESS:	It is not possible. I know that. It's never possible. An axle is broken. A horse is lamed. Always excuses.
STEWARD:	Not today, my lady.

(THE COUNTESS STARES AT HIM.)

COUNTESS:	Surely my carriage isn't ready? The first day since I have been here that I have no wish to view the countryside and suddenly my carriage is ready. What does this mean?
STEWARD:	Not your carriage, my lady.

(A SILENCE. THEN LOUISE ENTERS. THE STEWARD LEAVES)

LOUISE:	My carriage is at the door. I thought we might go for a drive.
COUNTESS:	Any particular reason?
LOUISE:	I'd like somebody to be with me.
COUNTESS:	Again I ask – any particular reason?
LOUISE:	Does there have to be one?
COUNTESS:	(RECOVERING) You're looking well, my dear. If a little over excited.
LOUISE:	I have been visiting someone.
COUNTESS:	Were his attentions pleasing to you?
LOUISE:	I was visiting an elderly lady of my acquaintance.
COUNTESS:	And your husband?
LOUISE:	He is out hunting.
COUNTESS:	In this weather?
LOUISE:	In any weather. (PAUSE) So I don't need to be at home just yet. Which is why on my way home I thought of you.
COUNTESS:	How kind.
LOUISE:	Not at all. I am very grateful for your tales. So do you want to come?
COUNTESS:	No, I know I sound ungrateful but – no.
LOUISE:	You seem upset.
COUNTESS:	I am – in a way. What about Philippe?
LOUISE:	What about him?
COUNTESS:	Is he out hunting too?
LOUISE:	I'm really not sure. (PAUSE) And what about your friend – may I enquire what has happened to her?
COUNTESS:	No, you may not. But if you are content to sit here with me, you may hear my new story.
LOUISE:	No one else has heard it?
COUNTESS:	I am still working upon it.

LOUISE:	Once upon a time there was a Queen–
COUNTESS:	No, a King – with <u>three</u> daughters. One who talked too much, one who was bone-idle and one who was–
LOUISE:	Intelligent and resourceful?
COUNTESS:	Just so. And surprisingly, despite her excellent qualities she was also her father's favourite.

(THE FANFARE. THE AGITATION IN THE FOLIAGE OF THE GARDEN.)
(THE KING AND FINETTA APPEAR.)

KING:	Finetta, my dear –
FINETTA:	Yes, father?
KING:	You know I am going off to war to fight the pagan?
FINETTA:	It is expected of kings like you, father.
KING:	Just so. But I have been concerned about how your sisters will behave during my absence so I have consulted an eminent fairy of my acquaintance on the subject. It's not that your sisters are undutiful but – neither of them is known for her prudence. And, well, it is important they come to no harm – if you understand me.
FINETTA:	So what has the fairy proposed, father?
KING:	Well, it's quite a drastic solution I'm afraid. You're all going to have to go and live in a high tower in a very secluded spot away from trouble–
FINETTA:	That's her advice?
KING:	I'm afraid so – because of your sisters. And while you're in that tower, no visitors are allowed.
FINETTA:	(POLITELY) No visitors and we're locked in – how are we going to eat, father?
KING:	Good question. There's going to be a pulley attached to one of the windows of the tower and provisions are going to be sent up to you every day by trusted servants.
FINETTA:	But I'm still concerned about my sisters. They're very loveable but easily lead astray.
KING:	Which is where the glass distaffs come in.
FINETTA:	Father, you lose me. Which glass distaffs?
KING:	Each of you will be given a glass distaff prepared by this very eminent fairy. If by any chance any of you girls does something that damages her honour then the relevant distaff will shatter into pieces. So – when I return – it will be clear how prudently you have – or have not -behaved.
FINETTA:	What will you do if all our distaffs are shattered?
KING:	Let's not think about that. I trust you, Finetta, to make sure it doesn't happen.
FINETTA:	(DRYLY) I appreciate your trust, father.

(MUSIC AS THE TOWER IS CONSTRUCTED AND THE THREE SISTERS AND THEIR GLASS DISTAFFS ARE INSTALLED AND LOCKED IN.)

COUNTESS:	The princesses were duly locked up in the tower with their glass distaffs and the King went off to war.

(FINETTA SITS READING WHILE BABILLARDA BUSTLES ABOUT AIMLESSLY AND IDELFONZA LANGUISHES.)

IDELFONZA:	Finetta, there's no one to help me! I'm supposed to do everything for myself.
FINETTA:	Father's orders, Idelfonza.
IDELFONZA:	(YAWNS) I know but I'm exhausted.
BABILLARDA:	And I'm so bored. There's no one to gossip about. There's no one to gossip to.
FINETTA:	It can't be helped, Babillarda.
BABILLARDA	But I feel as if I don't really exist.
FINETTA:	You'll just have to get used to it.

(AS FINETTA GOES OFF, WRAPPED IN HER BOOK, AN OLD WOMAN APPEARS BELOW THE TOWER. THIS IS PRINCE RICHCRAFT, MASTER OF DISGUISE.

RICHCRAFT:	(CALLING UP - AS THE OLD WOMAN) Oh princesses, lovely princesses, take pity on a poor old lady.
BABILLARDA::	Do you hear a voice, sister?
IDELFONZA:	(YAWNING) You know I think I do.
RICHCRAFT:	(STILL AS OLD WOMAN) Lovely princesses, do you need a loyal and energetic serving woman?
IDELFONZA:	I certainly do.
RICHCRAFT:	Do you want to hear all the latest gossip?
BABILLARDA:	I'm desperate for it. I'm going mad stuck in this tower. Lead me to the gossip – at once!

(BABILLARDA RUSHES TO THE EDGE OF THE TOWER AND PEERS DOWN AT THE OLD WOMAN.)

COUNTESS:	Of course, this old woman standing outside the tower was not an old woman at all. It was Prince Richcraft, the elder son of the King of the neighbouring kingdom and one of the most cunning individuals you were ever likely to meet. He saw the princesses in the tower as a challenge.

(THE OLD WOMAN SMILES ENCOURAGINGLY AT BABILLARDA.)

RICHCRAFT:	So you'd like me to come and work for you?
BABILLARDA:	Of course, of course. I'm deprived of proper conversation.
IDELFONZA:	(YAWNING) And I desperately need some help - I'm exhausted…

RICHCRAFT:	Then lower the basket you use for food and I'll come up and visit you-

(THE SISTERS HESITATE THEN BABILLARDA DECIDES AND GOES TO THE PULLEY.)
(THE BASKET CONTAINING THE OLD WOMAN IS SLOWLY PULLED UP.)
(AS IT REACHES THE TOP OF THE TOWER, THE OLD WOMAN GETS OUT. THE SISTERS LOOK AT HER EXPECTANTLY.)

RICHCRAFT:	(AS OLD WOMAN) Thank you, my dears.
BABILLARDA:	Welcome to our tower. So what's the news?
IDELFONZA:	Can you fetch me my gloves?
RICHCRAFT:	(REAL VOICE) I can do more than that, lovely princesses!

(HE THROWS OFF HIS DISGUISE AND REVEALS HIMSELF IN HIS OWN ELEGANT APPAREL.)

RICHCRAFT:	Prince Richcraft at your service.
BABILLARDA:	Oh!!!
IDELFONZA:	(LETHARGICALLY) Ohhh!!!
BABILLARDA	I must get help, Idelfonza. Finetta, Finetta, where are you?

(SHE RUNS OFF. IDELFONZA STIRS HERSELF TO FOLLOW BUT RICHCRAFT SWIFTLY STOPS HER.)

RICHCRAFT:	Oh, Princess, lovely Princess- hear me out, please!
IDELFONZA:	Who did you say you were?
RICHCRAFT:	The Prince Richcraft – who burns only with love for you. Don't you believe me?
IDELFONZA:	It's too much effort.
RICHCRAFT:	But it's your languorous, relaxed beauty that particularly excites my passion.
IDELFONZA:	I don't follow.
RICHCRAFT:	It's because you are so relaxed that I long to marry you.
IDELFONZA:	I beg your pardon?
RICHCRAFT:	I want to marry you!
IDELFONZA:	This is awfully sudden.
RICHCRAFT:	Not at all. I have heard of your beauty but only now have I had the opportunity to see it for myself. And I am entranced.
IDELFONZA:	Are you?
RICHCRAFT:	You know I am.
IDELFONZA:	Do I?
RICHCRAFT:	Oh yes. I want you to marry me.
IDELFONZA:	But-
RICHCRAFT:	You don't have the strength to say no, do you?
IDELFONZA:	Well, as a matter of fact, I don't.
RICHCRAFT:	So say you'll be mine, lovely Idelfonza.
IDELFONZA:	Oh… very well… I'll be yours.

RICHCRAFT:	(KISSING HER) My darling... Mmmm...
	(AS THEY KISS, THE LIGHTS FADE.) (THE SOUND OF SHATTERING GLASS. THE FIRST GLASS DISTAFF BREAKS.)
COUNTESS:	And with that kiss, the first glass distaff broke into a thousand pieces.
	(IDELFONZA SHRIEKS IN THE DARKNESS.) (RICHCRAFT COMES IN SEARCH OF THE OTHERS.)
COUNTESS:	Richcraft locked the traumatised Idelfonza in her room and went in search of the others, who had taken refuge in their respective rooms. It wasn't hard to locate Babillarda who in the absence of anyone else to talk to was talking to herself.
	(RICHCRAFT AND BABILLARDA ON EITHER SIDE OF A LOCKED DOOR. BABILLARDA IS MUTTERING TO HERSELF AS RICHCRAFT KNOCKS.)
RICHCRAFT:	Princess – excuse me, Princess –
BABILLARDA:	Who's there?
RICHCRAFT:	The Prince Richcraft.
BABILLARDA:	The Prince Richcraft! I can't possibly let you in here. Finetta warned me not to. But-
RICHCRAFT:	You'd like to talk?
BABILLARDA:	I'm going crazy in here with no one to talk to.
RICHCRAFT:	Then you must hear me – I am here for only one purpose. I am here to offer you my heart and hand.
BABILLARDA:	Your heart and hand! How terribly exciting! I've never had a proposal of marriage before because I'm the middle sister and, of course, Idelfonza should be married before I can possibly-
RICHCRAFT:	But it is you I love. You are so vivacious, so entertaining, so lovely. If only I could talk to you face to face, I could persuade you.
BABILLARDA:	I can't.
RICHCRAFT:	Don't you trust me - my beauteous, desirable Babillarda?
BABILLARDA:	I can't.
RICHCRAFT:	Then I shall have to leave you – the pain is too much.
BABILLARDA:	(FUMBLING WITH THE KEYS) But you can't go now. There's so many things I have to tell you. Like about the glass distaffs. There's so many things I have to ask you. There's-
RICHCRAFT:	(MAKING TO GO) No, no, goodbye-
	(BABILLARDA FINALLY OPENS THE DOOR)
BABILLARDA:	(EMERGING FROM HER ROOM) Come back!!!
RICHCRAFT:	Of course. (PAUSE) So tell me about those glass distaffs you mentioned.

BABILLARDA	Well, it's not much really and I suppose I shouldn't tell you but we've been left a glass distaff each and if – well, you know – if we misbehave then our distaffs shatter.
RICHCRAFT:	(TURNED ON BY THIS) They really shatter?
BABILLARDA	Oh yes, it's all nonsense, of course, but –
RICHCRAFT:	Lovely princess – I cannot contain myself any longer, much though I could listen to your talk for ever. Please - agree to be mine-
BABILLARDA:	But, Prince, you know I'd love to marry you but I've explained first it's Idelfonza then -
RICHCRAFT:	Hush, my lovely prattler – you don't want your elder sister to get me, do you?
BABILLARDA:	Of course not But-
RICHCRAFT:	Then will you be mine?
BABILLARDA:	Yes, oh yes.
RICHCRAFT:	Mmmmm…

(THEY KISS. AGAIN THEY DISAPPEAR INTO THE DARK.)
AGAIN THE SOUND OF SHATTERING GLASS. ANOTHER DISTAFF SHATTERS.)
(A SHRIEK OF DESPAIR FROM BABILLARDA.)
(A TRIUMPHANT RICHCRAFT AGAIN EMERGES FROM THE SHADOWS.)

COUNTESS:	Which, of course, only left Finetta with her glass distaff, as it were, intact.

(RICHCRAFT AND FINETTEA ON EITHER SIDE OF A DOOR. HE BATTERS HEAVILY ON IT.)

RICHCRAFT:	Princess – princess – let me in.
FINETTA:	Never!
RICHCRAFT:	Trust me!
FINETTA:	Never!
RICHCRAFT:	Pity me!
FINETTA:	Never!
RICHCRAFT:	Very well.

(HE SEIZES A LOG AND USES IT ON THE DOOR AS A BATTERING RAM. FINETTA LOOKS AROUND HER FOR A RESPONSE.)
(FINALLY RICHCRAFT RAMS THE DOOR IN AND BURSTS THROUGH TRIUMPHANTLY.)

RICHCRAFT:	So – lovely princess – at last we are face to face.

(AS HE ADVANCES TOWARDS HER, FINETTA PRODUCES A LARGE HAMMER.)

FINETTA:	Advance one step nearer, Prince, and I'll split your skull open.
RICHCRAFT:	But, lovely princess-
FINETTA:	I mean it!

(PAUSE. RICHCRAFT TRIES ANOTHER TACTIC.)

RICHCRAFT:	I am flattered, princess. I did not think the love I feel for you could inspire you with such hatred.
FINETTA:	Where are my sisters?
RICHCRAFT:	What do your sisters matter? It's you I care for.
FINETTA:	I need to see that they are all right.
RICHCRAFT:	Then agree to be mine.
FINETTA:	I cannot.
RICHCRAFT:	You don't know how lovely you look there. I cannot let you by unless you consent to be mine.

(FINETTA TRIES TO GET PAST. RICHCRAFT PRODUCES A SWORD AND BARS HER WAY.)

FINETTA:	(SLOWLY) If I agree to marry you, you will let me seek my sisters?
RICHCRAFT:	I give you my word of honour.

(THEY STARE AT EACH OTHER.)

FINETTA:	Then – handsome prince – I will gladly consent to marry you-
RICHCRAFT:	(TRIUMPHANTLY) Ah!
FINETTA:	But there is one condition. It is night-time now and I believe that marriages made at night always turn out to be unhappy. Would you be prepared to postpone the ceremony until tomorrow morning?
RICHCRAFT:	Is this necessary?
FINETTA:	It is to me. First I must find my sisters and make sure they are not harmed.
RICHCRAFT:	But-
FINETTA:	I promise to mention none of this to them – and then – after I have said my prayers - I promise to show you a very comfortable bed where you may spend the night-
RICHCRAFT:	And tomorrow morning?
FINETTA:	(SOFTLY) I will be waiting for you in my bedroom. Is it a bargain?
RICHCRAFT:	Yes, oh yes.

(AS FINETTA LEAVES, RICHCRAFT CASTS A LUSTFUL LOOK AFTER HER.)
(FINETTA FINDS HER TWO SISTERS IN TEARS.)

IDELFONZA:	Ohhh…
BABILLARDA:	I didn't mean to promise, Finetta, really I didn't.

FINETTA:	(WITH A SIGH) What's done cannot be mended. What rests to be done is another matter.
	(FINETTA ENTERS A DARKENED ROOM AND HER ACTIVITIES ARE DIMLY SEEN AS SHE WORKS AWAY.)
COUNTESS:	Finetta rushed into one of the rooms in the tower. It looked like the others but at its centre was a large hole through which all the rubbish and slops in the tower were disposed of down a very long tunnel. She put a couple of thin twigs across the hole and then made a clean bed on top of them.
	(THE CLEAN BED RESTS ENTICINGLY IN THE MIDDLE OF THE ROOM. A SMILING FINETTA USHERS RICHCRAFT IN)
FINETTA:	Here is your bed, prince.
RICHCRAFT:	Thank you.
FINETTA:	Sleep well.
RICHCRAFT:	Till tomorrow then.
FINETTA:	Till tomorrow.
	(SHE SMILES. HE BLOWS HER A KISS. FINETTA LEAVES.)
	(THOROUGHLY PLEASED WITH HIMSELF, RICHCRAFT YAWNS AND THROWS HIMSELF ON TO THE BED.)
	(IT PROMPTLY COLLAPSES UNDERNEATH HIM.)
	(HE SCREAMS AS HE DISAPPEARS.)
	(IN THE DARKNESS FURTHER SCREAMS AS A BODY IS HEARD SLITHERING DOWN A METALLIC TUNNEL.)
	(FINALLY AN ALMIGHTY THUMP.)
	(RICHCRAFT LIES BRUISED AND FURIOUS ON THE GROUND.)
RICHCRAFT:	Aaargh!!! Aaargh! Curse her! Curse her! Curse her!!! I'll have my revenge, Finetta, don't doubt it. I'll be back.
	(LIGHTS FADE ON THE GROANING RICHCRAFT.)
COUNTESS:	Meanwhile, Finetta's two sisters were plunged in gloom because of their broken distaffs.
	(THE DEJECTED SISTERS SIT ON TOP OF THE TOWER.)
IDELFONZA:	Ahhhhh…. I'm so tired…
BABILLARDA:	Ahhhhh… I can hardly speak.
	(A FRUITSELLER APPEARS BELOW WITH BOXES OF FRUIT. IT IS, OF COURSE, PRINCE RICHCRAFT.)

RICHCRAFT:	(CALLING OUT) Lemons! Pears! Apples! Plums!

(THE SISTERS GAZE DOWN HUNGRILY.)

BABILLARDA:	Oh, look, Idelfonza, such delicious fruit…
IDELFONZA:	Nobody's peeled me a grape for ages.
RICHCRAFT:	Can I interest the lovely ladies in boxes of my juicy plums and crunchy apples?
IDELFONZA:	Yes, please…
BABILLARDA	Of course, you can.
RICHCRAFT:	Then lower the pulley and we'll load the boxes on.

(THE PULLEY DESCENDS.)
(THE LIGHTS DIM. SUDDENLY THE SISTERS SCREAM IN TERROR.)

COUNTESS:	The boxes, of course, contained soldiers in the pay of Prince Richcraft. No sooner were they inside the tower than they seized the Princess Finetta and dragged her away.

(IN THE DARKNESS THE SISTERS CALL OUT:)

IDELFONZA and BABILLARDA: (AS ONE) Finetta! Finetta!

(FINETTA UNDER GUARD CONFRONTS RICHCRAFT. BY HIM IS A LARGE WOODEN BARREL)

RICHCRAFT:	Well, Princess, you are now in my power and I have every intention of repaying you for the trick you played on me. You will observe that we are at the top of a very, very high mountain.
FINETTA:	(TRYING TO BE BRAVE) Indeed.
RICHCRAFT:	You will also observe this barrel. It is lined inside with knives, razors and jagged nails.
FINETTA:	(PEERING INSIDE) So I see.
RICHCRAFT:	I do not like to be humiliated. And you are going to pay for my humiliation.
FINETTA:	I was defending my sisters and myself.
RICHCRAFT:	I don't care for your reasons. I am going to punish you in the way you deserve. We are going to put you inside this barrel and roll you down this mountain.
FINETTA:	(COOLLY) Are you sure the barrel is strong enough?
RICHCRAFT:	(CROSSLY) Of course it's strong enough.
FINETTA:	I very much doubt it.
RICHCRAFT:	Don't be absurd.
FINETTA:	You'll look a fool again if it isn't.
RICHCRAFT:	I am absolutely certain. But to be double sure –

(HE PUTS HIS HEAD INSIDE THE BARREL TO INSPECT IT. AS HE DOES SO, FINETTA QUICKLU PUSHES HIM INTO THE BARREL.)
(THEN WITH A DEFT KICK SHE SENDS IT HURTLING DOWN THE MOUNTAIN.)
(RICHCRAFT SCREAMS IN ANGUISH AS THE LIGHTS FADE.)

COUNTESS: The wounds Prince Richcraft sustained were fatal. The people of his country were secretly relieved as they were not looking forward to the reign of this treacherous and sadistic prince. Richcraft's younger brother, Prince Belavoir, however, was desolate.

(RICHCRAFT LIES GROANING ON HIS DEATH BED ATTENDED BY BELAVOIR.)

BELAVOIR: Oh, Richcraft, I grieve to see you like this. I would do anything to cure you. We have tried every remedy – every doctor –
RICHCRAFT: (IN AGONY) Brother, listen to me-
BELAVOIR: Of course.
RICHCRAFT: I'm dying-
BELAVOIR: No, no…
RICHCRAFT: Oh yes, I'm dying – despite all your loving care. But you know who is responsible-
BELAVOIR: Yes, but-
RICHCRAFT: There are no buts. Brother, since you love me, I want you to grant me my dying wish.
BELAVOIR: You know your wishes are sacred to me.
RICHCRAFT: Then I shall die contented-
BELAVOIR: I'm glad.
RICHCRAFT: Because I shall be revenged.
BELAVOIR: Brother, what do you mean?
RICHCRAFT: Once I am dead, I want you to ask the Princess Finetta to marry you.
BELAVOIR: But, brother-
RICHCRAFT: You're young and handsome. You'll have no difficulty in getting her to agree.
BELAVOIR: Brother, I cannot-
RICHCRAFT: Oh yes, you can. You have promised. And my dying wish is that you marry the Princess Finetta. And the moment she is yours, I want you to plunge a dagger into her heart.
BELAVOIR: (HORRIFIED) Brother!
RICHCRAFT: (WEAKENING) You promised me – on my deathbed. Remember?
BELAVOIR: But, Richcraft, consider-
RICHCRAFT: Remember…

(A DEATH RATTLE FROM RICHCRAFT. HE FALLS BACK ON THE BED.)

(BELAVOIR GIVES AN ANGUISHED CRY.)

COUNTESS: In the meantime, the King, the father of Finetta and her sisters, returned. He demanded to see the glass distaffs. And he saw two of them were broken.

(THE KING, HIS THREE DAUGHTERS AND THE TWO BROKEN DISTAFFS.)

KING: Don't lie to me, Idelfonza, Babillarda. I know all too well what this means.
BABILLARDA: But father- listen to me – please-
KING: Out of my sight!
IDELFONZA: (YAWNING) Father – please – don't upset me –
KING: I never want to see you again!
FINETTA: Father, please, listen. It wasn't their fault.
KING: Yes, it was. Only you remained true. Idelfonza – Babillarda – you are banished – to a parched desert land. I never want to set eyes on you again.

(THE TWO SISTERS GIVE A WAIL OF PROTEST.)
(LEFT ALONE, THEY ARE AT THE MERCY OF THE SAVAGE DESERT AIR.)

COUNTESS: Here in the unpitying desert Idelfonza soon died from heat and exhaustion. While Babillarda wasted her gossip on the desert air - before succumbing to misery and loneliness.

(THE SISTERS DISAPPEAR INTO NOTHINGNESS.)
(THE KING ADDRESSES HIS SURVIVING DAUGHTER.)

KING: Finetta, I forbid you to mourn.
FINETTA: But father –
KING: They are paying the price of their feminine frailty. Besides, I have something important to tell you. Prince Belavoir has requested your hand in marriage.
FINETTA: But father, I cannot marry him!
KING: That is not for you to say.
FINETTA: He is the brother of the Prince Richcraft-
KING: It is a highly suitable match.
FINETTA: How can I marry the brother of-
KING: I have decided that you will marry him.

(THE KING STOMPS OFF.)

COUNTESS: In those days, you see, the inclination of the partners was the last thing considered in arranging marriages. (DRYLY) How times change! (PAUSE) Anyway, some weeks later, the Princess was married to an ambassador in the name of Prince Belavoir and then she was lead over the border to meet her husband in his own country. As she had been directly responsible for the death of the heir to the throne, her qualms may be imagined. But when she saw Belavoir, all that changed.

(BELAVOIR AND FINETTA MEET EACH OTHER. RAMEAU'S DELICATE MUSIC INDICATES THAT THEY ARE IMMEDIATELY ATTRACTED TO EACH OTHER.)

BELAVOIR: Welcome, Finetta. Welcome, my bride.
FINETTA: Thank you, prince. Because of the past, I – I had not expected to feel like this.
BELAVOIR: I think I have the same feelings as you do. Ah, Finetta, if only -

(A SUDDEN PANIC CROSSES HIS FACE.)

FINETTA: If only what?
BELAVOIR: I cannot say. (PAUSE) How happy I could be with you if only -
FINETTA: If only what?
BELAVOIR: If only – (SADLY) No, best for you not to know.

(FINETTA GIVES HIM A SEARCHING LOOK.)

COUNTESS: Finetta liked the Prince enormously for his beauty and sweet nature. But everything she heard or noticed screamed caution. So before the nuptial night she sent for her faithful lady in waiting.

(FINETTA IN THE NUPTIAL BEDROOM WITH HER WAITING WOMAN.)

FINETTA: Alice, I need your help.
WAITING WOMAN: Are you in trouble, your highness?
FINETTA: I – I don't know. But I have to be sure. Bring me some straw-
WAITING WOMAN: Yes, your highness.
FINETTA: And bring me a bladder-
WAITING WOMAN: Yes, your majesty.
FINETTA: And some sheep's blood-
WAITING WOMAN: Yes, your majesty.
FINETTA: And the entrails of some of the animals prepared for supper-

(A LONG PAUSE. THE WAITING WOMAN DOES NOT BLINK.)

WAITING WOMAN: Will that be all, your highness?
FINETTA: (GENTLY) Yes, I think so.

(IN THE SEMI-DARKNESS FINETTA WORKS AWAY AT HER PLAN..)

COUNTESS:	Later, alone in the bridal chamber, Finetta made a figure out of the straw. Then she inserted into it the entrails and the bladder filled with blood. Then she dressed the figure she had created in her night dress and put it in the bed –

(WEDDING MUSIC. BELAVOIR AND FINETTA ARE ACCOMPANIED TO THE DOOR OF THE NUPTIAL ROOM BY CHEERS.)
(FINETTA KISSES BELAVOIR.)

FINETTA:	Give me a few moments – to prepare myself.
BELAVOIR:	Of course, my love.

(THEY STARE AT EACH OTHER DEEPLY TROUBLED.)
(THEN FINETTA DISAPPEARS INTO THE ROOM.)
(THE PRINCE WAITS IN AGONY.)

FINETTA:	(SOFTLY - FROM THE DARKNESS) Belavoir!

(THE PRINCE ENTERS THE SEMI-LIT ROOM. ON THE BED LIES A WAITING FIGURE. HE IS CLOSE TO TEARS AS HE PULLS OUT HIS SWORD.)

BELAVOIR:	Oh, Finetta, Finetta, this is not my wish. But I promised my brother on his death-bed. How much I have wanted to love and cherish you from the first moment I saw you. Even in my brother's account, you showed courage and discretion. The last thing I wish to do is kill you but I have no choice. Farewell, my love.

(HE STARTS TO STAB THE FIGURE ON THE BED.)
(BLOOD SPURTS OUT. HE STABS AGAIN AND AGAIN CRYING AS HE DOES SO. MORE BLOOD SPURTS FROM THE BODY)

(SUDDENLY THE STEWARD ENTERS THE GARDEN, FULL OF BREATHLESS SELF-IMPORTANCE.)
(THE PRINCE AND THE BODY IMMEDIATELY DISAPPEAR. THE COUNTESS AND LOUISE SIT ALONE.)

STEWARD:	My lady, there's somebody asking to speak to Madame de Ventadour.

(A YOUNG MAN ENTERS THE GARDEN. THE STEWARD LEAVES.)

PHILIPPE:	Ladies, forgive me for bursting in like this.
LOUISE:	Philippe, what is the matter?
PHILIPPE:	Madame, I'm afraid there has been a terrible accident-
LOUISE:	An accident! What do you mean?

PHILIPPE: Your husband, the Count, while out hunting-
LOUISE: He is not dead?
PHILIPPE: Madame, I am sorry-
LOUISE: (CRYING OUT) Oh no, no!

(SHE GIVES A LITTLE SIGH AND COLLAPSES IN A FAINT.)

COUNTESS: Well, you know how to make an entry, Monsieur.
PHILIPPE: Forgive me, Madame. I-
COUNTESS: Spare your apologies, we must attend to Madame de Ventadour.

(THEY HELP LOUISE TO A SEAT.)

COUNTESS: It's all right, Louise, we're here.

(LOUISE STARTS TO COME TO.)

LOUISE: My husband! It cannot be true!

(SHE FAINTS AGAIN.)

PHILIPPE: (TO LOUISE) Madame, I feel so guilty. I hate to be the bringer of bad news.
COUNTESS: Don't overdo it, young man.
PHILIPPE: (STARTLED) What do you mean?
COUNTESS: What exactly happened?
PHILIPPE: A terrible accident.
COUNTESS: So you said.
PHILIPPE: To do with his stirrups.
COUNTESS: Something was faulty with the stirrups?
PHILIPPE: Yes.
COUNTESS: So how long have you been in the service of Madame de Ventadour?
PHILIPPE: (STIFFLY) I am in the service of Monsieur her husband, Madame.
COUNTESS: You were in his service - how long?
PHILIPPE: Three years.
COUNTESS: And he is -was- a good master?
PHILIPPE: We are all devoted to him. This terrible accident is a great shock to us all.
COUNTESS: So the stirrups were not properly secured?
PHILIPPE: Monsieur is -was- an excellent rider. There is no other explanation for how he could have fallen as he did.
COUNTESS: Who is responsible for checking the stirrups?
PHILIPPE: A well trusted groom who has served Monsieur for a number of years.
COUNTESS: So nobody else could have tampered with them?
PHILIPPE: But, Madame, why would anybody want to do that?

COUNTESS:	I've no idea. Did anybody else have access?
PHILIPPE:	The Count was adamant that nobody else came near. It can only have been that he readjusted them himself incorrectly.
COUNTESS:	And there is no doubt his neck is broken?
PHILIPPE:	(TEARFULLY) Madame, the best medical help had been summoned before I came here to find Madame. But it was useless. This is terrible news to bring to Madame, I know. They were a devoted couple.
COUNTESS:	So she told me.
PHILIPPE:	It is fortunate that she was here with you.
COUNTESS:	She seemed very keen I should take a drive with her, it's true. But whether I'm the right person to be with at such a moment is a matter of opinion.
PHILIPPE:	Madame?
COUNTESS:	My poor boy, how could you know that I have a reputation when it comes to husbands?

(LOUISE STARTS TO COME TO.)

LOUISE:	Madame, I am so sorry.
COUNTESS:	Are you feeling better?
LOUISE:	I – I think I should perhaps return home.
COUNTESS:	I think so too.
LOUISE:	(TEARFUL) My poor Henri! It's like some awful nightmare! I cannot believe this has happened. It's like a nightmare, isn't it, Philippe?
PHILIPPE:	It is difficult to imagine a future without the Count.

(A LOOK OF UNDERSTANDING BETWEEN THEM.)

LOUISE:	Madame-
COUNTESS:	Yes?
LOUISE:	You never finished your story.
COUNTESS:	That is not important now.
LOUISE:	I should like to know what happened. (PAUSE) I need to know.
COUNTESS:	Very well.

(SUDDENLY BELAVOIR IS BACK STABBING FRANTICALLY AT THE BLOODY CORPSE.)
(AT LAST MENTALLY AND PHYSICALLY EXHAUSTED, HE STOPS.)

BELAVOIR:	What have I done! Oh, what have I done! Oh, brother, why did I promise you to kill her when I loved her so much.

(HE STARTS TO CRY.)

BELAVOIR:	Finetta, oh, Finetta!

(OUT OF THE SHADOWS FINETTA APPEARS.)

FINETTA:	Do not grieve, Prince. I am not dead. Forgive me for playing you a trick which saved you from committing a crime–
BELAVOIR:	And saved your life! How could I reproach you, my far-sighted darling!
FINETTA:	My prince!
BELAVOIR:	My princess!

(THEY EMBRACE. THE POLYMNIE MUSIC RETURNS AS THE LIGHTS FADE ON THEM AGAIN.)

COUNTESS: And so the Prince and Princess lived happily ever after and everyone sang the praises of the discreet princess.

(A LONG PAUSE.)

LOUISE:	I'm glad it had a happy ending.
COUNTESS:	You approve?
LOUISE:	Idelfonza did nothing. Babillarda talked too much. Finetta deserved to survive.
COUNTESS:	Better to be energetic and discreet–
LOUISE:	Just so. And not trust people too much.
COUNTESS:	There is that as well.
LOUISE:	(GLANCING AT PHILIPPE) There are things I would like to tell you.
COUNTESS:	Best not.
LOUISE:	You see, your fairy tales showed me–
COUNTESS:	Believe me, best not. Let us just say – perhaps in the end I was your Fairy Godmother.
PHILIPPE:	Do you feel able to walk, madame?
LOUISE:	Oh yes.
PHILIPPE:	Then let me lead you to your carriage.

(HE TAKES HER HAND.)
(THE GARDEN QUIVERS AS THEY GO)
(AS THEY REACH THE ENTRANCE TO THE GARDEN, LOUISE TURNS BACK.)

LOUISE:	Goodbye, Madame.
COUNTESS:	Goodbye, my dear.

(LOUISE AND PHILIPPE LEAVE.)
(THE GARDEN IS QUIET.)
(THE COUNTESS STANDS THERE, SUDDENLY VERY ALONE AND DESOLATE.)

COUNTESS: I imagine their happy ending. But for me?

(A LONG PAUSE.)

(THEN THE POLHYMNIE MUSIC STARTS TO PLAY AGAIN.)
(THE STEWARD ENTERS – WEARING A PAIR OF LARGE GOLDEN WINGS AND CARRYING A LETTER.)

COUNTESS: A pardon? From his Majesty? For me?

(THE STEWARD NODS THEN HANDS THE LETTER TO THE COUNTESS AND DEPARTS.)
(THE COUNTESS READS THE LETTER AND A SMILE SPREADS OVER HER FACE.)

COUNTESS: Oh, my dear Eloise, how delightful to learn that at long last I may return.

(RAMEAU'S MUSIC STARTS TO PLAY.)

COUNTESS: I have written several new stories which I look forward to reading to you all. Indeed, I cannot tell you how much I long for the innocence of Paris…

(THE GARDEN PULSATES WITH LIFE.)
(THE COUNTESS STANDS THERE, ECSTATIC, AS THE LIGHTS FADE AND RAMEAU'S MUSIC PLAYS.)

THE END

www.ingramcontent.com/pod-product-compliance
Ingram Content Group UK Ltd.
Pitfield, Milton Keynes, MK11 3LW, UK
UKHW041959230426
12048UKWH00008B/417